THE GREAT CATSBY

A SAM THE CAT MYSTERY

FOR INFORMATION ABOUT THESE TITLES
please contact:
CHESHIRE HOUSE BOOKS
P.O. Box 2484, New York, New York 10021
or look for Sam's web site:
HTTP://WWW.SAMTHECAT.COM

THE
GREAT
CATSBY

LINDA STEWART

CHESHIRE HOUSE BOOKS
NEW YORK

COPYRIGHT © 2013, BY LINDA STEWART

CHESHIRE HOUSE BOOKS
P.O. Box 2484
New York, New York 10021

COVER ILLUSTRATION: Sam Ryskind

DESIGN & PRODUCTION: Bernard Chase

ISBN 978-0-9675073-6-1

LIBRARY OF CONGRESS CATALOG CARD NUMBER
2013931081

THE GREAT CATSBY

A SAM THE CAT MYSTERY

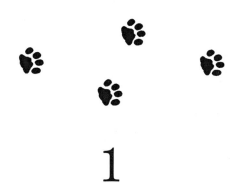

1

The first time I saw Catsby he was sitting atop a diving board and staring across a swimming pool at a lantern hung from a tree. It was one of those green paper Japanese lanterns and it flashed, in the local distance, like the light of an alien star. Of course I didn't know he was Catsby then, or anything else about him. By his looks, he was nothing special— just a pleasantly yellow fellow with a curve at the tip of his tail. What impressed me had been his gaze— an almost laser-like concentration— and the stillness that seemed to surround him the way a halo surrounds a saint. I didn't call to him. Catsby's stillness gave me the feeling of being in church, and even I, tactless and brassy, wouldn't hassle a man at prayer. So I skipped the greeting and walked away.

It was 10 o'clock in the morning on the first weekend of summer or the last weekend of spring, and I'd been kidnapped to Long Island or, more precisely, to East Ham. There are two of them — two Hams, nestled neatly around a bay. The one in the east is the one you've heard of— that celebrity-studded sandbox where the rock stars and realtors play, and the Wall Street wizards, still making trillions in tentative dollars, come out to be cool.

I had *not* wanted to be here. (I had not been given a choice.) Hunnicker, the guy I share my office with in the city, had been invited to stay with his sister, and said sister— she of the hideous jangling bracelets and reeking perfume— had alas convinced him, through constant nagging, that "country air" would be good for "the cat."

So here I was in a foreign "country," digging my paws into foreign soil, and wondering vaguely what would be "good." Chasing butterflies doesn't move me. Climbing trees can be good for an hour, but after that, in a manner of speaking, it's all bark and no bite. Lucky for me, there were other options.

I had a cousin in East Ham. I'd only seen her a couple of times, back in the days when she'd lived in Manhattan, but Pansy was famous, or practically so. Her famous roommate was Rex Trout. Never heard of him? Good for you. Trout was famous for dishing dirt. For several decades he'd ladled it out for a local tabloid with national clout— celebrities trembled whenever he neared— but I guess he'd retired to his place in the country. Rumor had it he'd gotten canned but I'd never read him and didn't care except about Pansy. Very sincerely I'd always hoped she was doing well.

I hadn't thought that I'd get to see her till several days ago in the city. My good friend Sue had discovered her picture, along with Rex's, in *Vanity Fair*, and been nearly a-twitter. "Sammy, Sammy! Look at your cousin!" She showed me the shot. And there was Pansy, delicate flower, gaily bejeweled and satiny-white, in the muscular arms of the aging Trout. "So then if you *do* have to go to the country—"

"I plan on hiding," I said.

"In the country?"

"I mean in the city. Under the desk or behind a bookshelf or under the rug. When he gets the carrier out, I'm over. Up in the attic. Gone with the wind. I'm never going," I said.

"Uh-huh. And then when you get there, Featherstone Road. That's what it says here, Sammy. 'Rexford and Pansy Trout of Featherstone Road.'"

Which left me looking for Featherstone Road in the wooded wonders of East Ham. I started off through a leafy forest— a small collection of birch and pine that bordered closely on Hunnicker's house, but after minutes I seemed to be lost. There was nothing useful around to guide me. Nothing doing except for trees. And beyond the trees, there were other trees. I saw a robin flit through the air. I heard a chipmunk, making a suddenly serious sound of soprano shrieks, and I saw a hawk, circling slowly, looking for breakfast, dinner, or me. This was rapidly getting creepy. This was not, I decided, "good." I stopped advancing and looked around. I looked for witches with open ovens. I looked for wolves with suspicious hoods. I figured out I was ready to scrap it—I could work my way back to Hunnicker's and pretend to enjoy the porch— and then I spotted the cat in the tree.

From far above me, I heard a sound— the subtle sound of a silent cat: a twitching whisker, a tapping tail. I perked my ears up and scanned the sky— a bright umbrella of limbs and leaves— and there he was, glowering greenly, lying extended across a branch as though he'd been sleeping and dreaming Dog; he wasn't smiling. I said, "Hello?"

"Go back where you came from," he spat. "Beat it. You city slickers are all the same. You come out to the country, you act like snobs."

"I wasn't acting," I said, "at all. Didn't even see you."

"That's what I mean." He flicked his tail in a nasty drumbeat. "Hear me, Slicker," he said, "get lost."

I started laughing. "I already am."

"Well it serves you right, Little Slicker, don't it. Come here flashin' your city ways and your—"

"Hold your horses!"

"That's what I mean."

I squinted up at him, craning my neck and scratching my shoulder. "*What's* what you mean?"

"'Hold your horses,'" he said. "You order your friends in the city to hold their horse? Or you ask em politely to hold their limo?"

"Can we start this over?" I said. "Listen. I've only *been* here for over an hour. I haven't snooted or snobbered anyone. I'm a stranger lost in the woods and I'm trying to get to my cousin Pansy's and—"

"Hold your teacup," he said. "Or your opera cape, or whatever you slickers hold. You mean to say you're the lady's cousin?"

"That's what I said and that's what I meant."

"Then why'nt you say so? All this lollygaggin' and fancy-dancin' around. Get your tail up here and I'll show you."

I looked suspiciously up at the tree. A country tree

4

is a no-kidding tree. The trees in the city are mostly kidding. They're short and slender and easy to climb, but this was a challenge. I took the bait. I hurled myself upward, taking the leap but it only propelled me to mid trunk where I dug my claws in and looked for something— anything!— solid to leap to next. The nearest limb was a mile away but I gauged the distance and then, *shazam!* Another *shazam* or two and I landed, flat on a limb at a glorious height, and a foot from my neighbor who gave me a wink.

"Well, you ain't a sissy," he said. "Them other lazy slickers, they wouldn't climb if you paid em catnip."

"You got any catnip?"

"I had any catnip, I wouldn't share."

"I didn't think so," I said, and grinned.

"The name'd be Virgil," he offered.

"Sam."

We looked at each other through leafy air. My reluctant Virgil was solidly built, entirely silver, and middle aged or perhaps older— about fourteen— but he wore it wisely and handled it well.

"Got a bird's-eye view here," he said. I looked, and pretended briefly to be a hawk. Far in the distance, over the treetops and over the rooftops, I saw the bay with its little sailboats and soaring gulls. Skimming the shoreline, I saw the houses— some of them tiny and some grotesque. There were Norman castles and crummy copies of Grecian temples and Swiss chalets, and modern barns made of shiny metals and glaring panels of winking glass.

"So them's your slickers," he said. "They settle theirselves in the country, they crud the view. Back in the old days— afore they come with their show-

5

off mansions— the shore was clear. You could sit in this treetop, my grandmama told me, you'd look real sharply, you'd see to France."

"That must've been something," I said.

"Dunno. I wasn't born yet. Neither was she."

"So your family's lived here for—"

"Mostly ever. Or close enough to it," Virgil announced. "The first of us come with the Dutch sailors. That'd be nigh on to five-hundred years and there's nothin around here but birds and bay and a couple of fish you could pull with your teeth." He lifted his glance from the ruined view. "About Miss Pansy," he said. "A wonderful beautiful lady. Convey my regards."

"I'll be happy to do that," I said. "If I get there."

"Oh you'll get there. You see that house?" He jerked his chin at a yellow cottage a half a mile or so from the tree. There were trees in front of it, bay behind. "There's a little road there. See where it angles? That'd be—"

"Featherstone?"

"That'd be that. And you best get going," he said. "Not to be took unkindly, I need a nap."

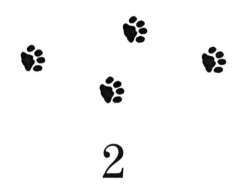

2

I couldn't help it. I think I was humming something like "Follow the Featherstone Road" as I crossed the forest and hung a left. Featherstone Road was a two-lane highway, narrow and curving and flanked by trees, and it quickly arrived at a wooden mailbox, set by the roadside and labeled TROUT. Over the mailbox, one of the trees had a Japanese lantern lit by the sun and it glittered greenly among the leaves— marking the mailbox, I thought, for inattentive mailmen and muddled guests. A gravel driveway led from the mailbox, passing a pasture of dewy lawn where it offered a gravel hook to the house.

Pansy's house was a fisherman's cottage, painted yellow with ivied walls and a wooden porch that was painted white. There were white shutters beside the windows which flaunted their panes at invading bugs and, not incidentally, invading cats. Perhaps in the rear, I thought, there'd be something conveniently open or partly ajar.

The back of the house had a view for the ages—the Dutch shoreline that Virgil missed. At the edge of the lawn was a dirt pathway that led, in one way, up to the house and led in the other one down to the bay. A wooden rowboat, docked at the shoulder, bobbed and bobbled beneath a tree.

I took the pathway up to the house. A central doorway welcomed me warmly, providing a cat-door that led to a hall where I landed intact on a wooly carpet. I heard some voices— Pansy's was one— and I followed the whisperings out through the hall and into a brightly attractive room that seemed to be furnished in solid white: white tables and white chairs and a pair of creamy upholstered sofas ringed by more of those shaggy rugs. My cousin Pansy lay on a sofa, nearly blending into its arm, as she whispered urgently to a stranger—a young Persian of palest yellow who looked indulgent and slightly bored.

Pansy heard me and partly rose and then laughed delightedly. "Why, it's Sam! It's my cousin Sammy!" she said and turned to her pale companion, who didn't care. Nevertheless, we were introduced. The blonde boredom was tagged as Georgia. Georgia tilted her head and yawned.

"You're the private detective," she finally managed. "Pansy mentioned you just today. After I told her she'd better find one."

"Why would she need one?" I looked at Pansy who suddenly furrowed her pretty brow. To call her "pretty" is insufficient. There's a sweetness about my cousin, something terribly close to angelic, and she knows it and plays it well. For a fleeting moment, her blue eyes darkened, shadowed deeply with midnight fear.

8

"What would you say," she began, "if I told you—" she broke it off and looked at the wall where a grandfather clock had been ticking grimly— "if I told you—" she stopped again, and the noisy seconds ticked like a bomb— "that I'm going to be— that I'm going to be *murdered* this weekend?"

"I'd tell you," I said quickly, "to go away for the weekend."

Georgia laughed at it. Pansy didn't.

"You're not serious, Pansy, are you? I mean... who'd want to murder *you*?"

She shrugged her shoulders and bowed her head.

It was total nonsense, of course. She didn't need a detective, just reassurance. Still, the only way I could give it was to pretend to be playing along. So I got the detective look on my face and said intently, "What makes you think so?"

"The dead flounder," she said. "And the duck."

I let it lay there and said, "Uh-*huh*," and, after a second, I said, "Go on."

"But you must be starving!" she suddenly babbled. "Where are my manners? I'll get you a treat." And before I could stop her, she bounded away and into the kitchen.

I watched her go. I'd held my ground on the shaggy carpet, afraid I'd leave my prints on the couch, but Georgia patted the cushion beside her. "Come and sit with me, private eye, and I'll tell you a secret." Her voice was low with the promised thrill of a naughty truth.

I wiped my paws off and made the leap. Not for the secret; just for the cushion. Secrets are shabby; the cushion was new.

"It's about poor Pansy," she said, "and Tom." She snuggled closer, touching my arm, and gave me the edge of a meaningful look whose meaning evaded me.

"Tom who?"

"I thought you'd met him. Or maybe not. Come to think of it," Georgia thought, "he never stayed with the Trouts in the city, just in the country."

"He lives here now?"

"When the spirit moves him. You know they're engaged. I mean Tom and Pansy."

I said, "That's swell. It's a secret engagement?"

She rolled her eyes. "The engagement's public," she said. "The *secret* is that Tom has another girl."

"And Pansy knows it?"

"Pansy suspects. I'll bet he's with her this very second." Georgia glanced through the sunny panes, casting her eyes on the wider world where advanced betrayals were taking place. "I mean even now," she said, "as we cat."

"And this is connected to Pansy's—"

"Ssh!" Georgia kicked me to shut me up as Pansy entered, daintily holding a packet of Pounces between her teeth. She dropped it artfully onto the cushion where it opened and sprang its load.

"So out with it, Pansy," I said, chomping. "About the duck, I mean, and the fish."

Her eyes grew darker again and she sighed. "They were both murdered," she said with feeling. "Their lifeless bodies dumped at the door."

"The duck and the flounder," I said.

"At the door. It started a week ago. No, it was two. It was two weeks ago Saturday morning. Mrs. Krapotkin arrived at the door and she—"

"Mrs. Krapotkin being?"

"The maid. She only comes here on Saturday mornings, except for this one, of course, when she's not on account of the holiday." Pansy paused. "It was totally dreadful," she said. "She finds this horrific flounder dead on the porch."

"Was it wrapped in paper?" I said. "In a bag?"

"It was stark naked," Pansy pronounced. "It was staring glassily up at the ceiling, cold as Christmas, and stinky dead. And the following weekend, she found the duck."

"Dead on the doorstep?"

"Hung by its neck."

I thought it over. Someone was either delivering suppers for Mr. Trout or sending a message. I scratched my ear. "Did you find a letter," I said, "or a note? Along with the corpses?"

"Not that I know."

"And about the flounder," I said, "are you certain the fish was a flounder and not a trout?"

It seemed to stop her. In fact, she gasped. "Oh my goodness," she said. "I don't know. The only fishes I know are in cans. But I'm almost certain that Mrs. Krapotkin—"

"Flounders are roundish and trouts are thin."

She cast her eyes up, imagining flounders. Then she looked at me. "No. A trout."

"And was Trout afraid of it?"

"Beg your pardon?"

"Did Trout, the person, see trout, the fish? And how did he take it?"

"Oh. He laughed. And Mrs. Krapotkin was fairly weeping. 'Oh my goodness,' she kept repeating. 'Oh my goodness, what does it *mean*?' "

"And what do *you* think it means, Pansy?"

"I think it means I'm the next to go. Like in all those stories, you know. Where somebody's actually after the family cat but they're trying to frighten her first with a fish. It's a kind of warning," she sighed, "to me."

"It's a kind of warning, all right. To Trout. Or, to make it plainer, I'll say 'to Rex.' Unless it isn't, of course."

"Isn't?"

"Perhaps it's only a practical joke. The thing to look for would be a motive. Why would somebody threaten Trout?"

"You've got to be kidding," Georgia exploded. "I can't b*elieve* that you wouldn't know." She looked at Pansy as though to say to her "who's this hick from the big city?" Then she leapt from the creamy couch and crossed to a spot at the edge of the room where a folded newspaper lay on the floor. She pawed the pages, shredding a couple and leaving them scattered in grizzly array till she finally stopped at whatever she wanted. "I'd bring it over," she said, "but I gag at the taste of newspaper. Come and look."

3

The shredded paper, spread on the floor, was a local rag called *The Ham Herald*, and what she referred me to with her paw was a shredded page from "Society News.":

HOTLY AWAITED NOVEL NOW READY FOR PUBLICATION

Trout Tell-All "Fiction" Finally Tells All

Herald Exclusive, May 23— *Some of My Best Friends,* the long-awaited novel by dirt-digging columnist Rex Trout, has apparently been completed, 5 years overdue. The book, for which Trout has collected, in advance, nearly half a million dollars, has continually been the subject of gossipy speculation, dealing, as it does, with the heartbreaks and scandals of— as he puts it— some of his best friends.

Thinly disguised as fiction, the book, we've been promised, will reveal a lot of utterly none-of-our-business dirt about half-a-dozen people— major celebrities of Hollywood and Manhattan, who also just happen to have homes in East Ham.

According to sources close to the publisher,

the manuscript ("of which," he said, "nobody's seen a word,") will be handed to its editor, Marietta Snidely, on the Saturday evening of Memorial Day weekend—

I was thunderstruck: that's tonight!

—at a gathering at the home of Mr. J.J. Smythington of Parvenu Road. At the same celebration, Mr. Trout will be reading a selected chapter in which one of six people will have his— or maybe her— dark secrets laid bare.

I thought slowly about the article and all I could say was "So." It occurred to me then and there that Pansy really could be in danger—left for dead on her own doorstep like a final and furry note: *Stop the blabbering/ Final Notice*. Heavy-hearted, I paced the floor.

"So...*what*?" Pansy said impatiently.

"Somebody wants him to burn the book."

"Or else they'll murder him?"

"That's the threat."

"But you said 'somebody,'" Georgia prodded. "I suppose you couldn't say who?"

I said, "Who."

She said, "What?"

I said, "You asked could I say 'who.'"

"Are you a moron," she said, "or what?"

"He was simply saying," Pansy injected, "that he doesn't know who it is. You couldn't *expect* him to know who it is. I mean, the question was kind of silly so the answer was silly too."

Georgia glared at her.

"Now, now," I said, "it wasn't silly as that. We could probably narrow it down. Figure it's one of the six people our blabbering author put in the book. Or else

14

it's one of a million people who's simply *scared* that he's in the book." I looked at Pansy. "Who's in the book?"

Pansy shrugged at me. "How would I know?"

"You've never read it?"

"Why would I read it? It's just about people." She shrugged contempt. "And besides all *that*," she admitted frankly, "I've been totally barred from the den. That's where he works on it."

"Where's the den?"

She gestured sideways, off to the left. The door was open.

"And where's he now?"

"He went to the doctor."

"He's feeling sick?"

"He simply went for his annual checkup."

"Annual checkups can take forever." I let it hang there. She picked it up and examined it slowly. She said, "I guess."

"And I guess I'll be leaving you," Georgia announced. "I'd better get home or my roommate'll kill me.— Speaking of murder," she giggled. And left.

Trout's office was small and clean, with most of the furniture made of oak. There wasn't much of it: desk, bookshelves, table, cabinet— that, and a chair. No computer! Atop the desk, was a very ancient battered machine— a Royal Portable— possibly dating back to the 'forties or even more. A manual typewriter!

"Holy rats!" I jumped to the desktop and circled around.

"Is something the matter?" Pansy was prowling the patterned carpet and looking scared.

"There's no hard drive," I muttered softly. "No

15

hard drive and no discs."

She looked at me crossly. "I have absolutely *no* idea what you mean."

"That the book's on paper," I said. "And aside from whatever he Xeroxed or—"

"Never mind. Can we get this over with?" Pansy said. "What are we looking for?"

"Well...the book. It would look like a manuscript—lots of pages with lots of typing. Say, in a box."

I looked around but there wasn't a box. A sunlit window flooded the room with the color of summer and summer fun, but it wasn't helpful. It showed me the shelves with the glossy photos and dusty books and the little table, off to the side, with a flashy fax machine and a pen. It showed me a cabinet (maybe with files—a couple of drawers of them; worth a look) and the meaningless items that covered the desk: the usual telephone, digital answerer, leather appointment book, halogen lamp. The desk, however, had five drawers. The one in the center was locked with a key that was pretty much pointlessly left in the lock.

"Take a look in the cabinet, Pansy," I said. "Look for a file that's as fat as a book." I turned my attention back to the key. I grabbed it lightly between my teeth and the drawer came open.

I saw a gun. It was fairly large as revolvers go—a Smith and Wesson, a .45. I sniffed the barrel. The gun was cold and hadn't been fired, or not in a while. It was lying lengthwise across the bed of a white envelope, hiding the print except for a patch on the upper left where a greenish-blueish globe of the world floated on yellow and sprouted wings. There were several bullets, loose in a box that was labeled "Paper Clips #1," and a couple of pencils that seemed to be chewed. I looked at them bleakly and closed the drawer.

The drawers on the sides were a disappointment. A messy collection of odds and ends— of dull pencils and rubber bands, of Royal ribbons and metal clips. Another drawer held some spiral notebooks—about a dozen— piled in a stack. In still another, a plastic checkbook with many envelopes sent by a bank, and a paper atlas, and nothing else.

I glanced at Pansy, who'd disappeared in the open shell of a cabinet drawer. "Anything doing?"

"Totally nothing." She rested her chin on the edge of the drawer. "Newspaper clippings," she spluttered, "and dust."

"And the drawer underneath it?"

She leapt to the floor.

"Had newspaper clippings," she spluttered, "and dust." She was staring dejectedly down at her paws. "Am I terribly horribly covered with dust?"

"You're a little gray-ish," I said. "Like me."

"You're a *lot* gray-ish," she mourned. "It's not that there's anything wrong with it if you're gray..."

"I think you'll recover," I said. In truth, I happen to like the fact that I'm gray: I don't show dust and I blend with shadows which works out nicely for shadowing crooks. "Meanwhile," I said, getting back to business, "there's only one other drawer I can check and after that we should look at the bedroom—"

"And after that?"

"I suggest we leave."

Pansy stared at me. "What do you mean?"

"I mean I think you'll be safer with me. Just till this evening," I said, reassuringly. "Once he's gone public, there's nothing to fear."

She nodded grimly. I opened the drawer: A pair of candles, a Ham phonebook, a high school yearbook from Ozark High. I was still considering Ozark High when a crackling splash on the gravel driveway shattered the silence and ended the search. It was Rex's Lexus, Pansy announced, and we made it out of there faster than fleas.

4

Pansy refused to go into the forest. "But what about lions and tigers and bears?"

I shook my head patiently. "Pansy, Pansy." I'd carefully covered the list of her fears and assured her exactly and one by one that there weren't dragons or wicked witches or giant ogres or slithering snakes or squishy squashes or moldy monsters or creepy crawlies or poisonous warts.

"Well what about—"

"*Pansy*," I said, "come on!" I trotted away from her into the shadows and, as I suspected, she followed along. For a time she was silent, building her courage and picking her way around smooth little stones, till a funny thing happened. The same yellow cat that I'd seen on the diving board fell from a tree. (Though jumped or fell would remain uncertain.) Still, whichever it was, he ker-plunked himself directly onto our path, quickly righted himself with dignity and then stuttered pitifully: "Beh-Beh-Beh-*Beh*-Beh-Beh-Begging your pardon. T-Terribly sorry."

I said, "It's okay."

The guy was staring directly at Pansy whose blue eyes widened with shock and awe and suddenly Pansy was stuttering too. "Cuh-Cuh-Cuh-*Cats*by?" she gasped.

"Puh-Pansy?"

I looked at the two of them, scratching my head. They were simply staring, each at the other, one of those magical mystical stares that if this were a movie you'd hear violins. I made a harumphing sound in my throat and they seemed to notice me.

"Cousin Sam, this is Mr. Catsby," Pansy recited.

I looked him over and gave him a "Hi."

He nodded distractedly. "Yes, we're neighbors. I live at the Smythington place—over there." He gestured behind him, leaving his eyes directly on Pansy. "Perhaps," he said, "you'd like to come over and look at the house?"

"Oh that would be lovely," Pansy accepted. "Wouldn't it, Sammy? Wouldn't it just?"

In fact I was eager to look at the house (where Trout would be reading tonight, if he lived) but I'd rather have scouted it out on my own.

"I'd just be intruding," I said. "It looks as though you and Catsby are—"

"Ancient friends. We met in the city. Ever so long ago," Pansy prattled. "When we were young. Why, I haven't seen him in—"

"Thirty-eight months," he injected quickly, "and seventeen hours and twenty-one days.— Let me show you a shortcut." He led the way through a bristly hedge at the edge of the woods and we entered a totally different planet— a scented garden as green and vast as a country meadow or palace park. At the end of the garden, I saw the pool where I'd first seen Catsby atop the board, and remembered the lantern— Pansy's lantern— the one he'd stared at with such regard.

He led us speedily past the house— a thing of limestone and leaded windows which wasn't larger than Grand Central Station— and gestured us happily into a hut that was planted firmly amid the flowers. It was Catsby's playroom. His own room! It was simply furnished: a feathered bed and a padded cat tree that climbed the wall and a wooden toy chest that sat on a rug surrounded by wallsful of colorful birds and a sunny window that looked on the lawn. Pansy was dazzled. "Oh my goodness. I've never *never*..." was all she could say.

"And I've got some catnip," he said. "And then I've a man at PetCo who makes me these." He strutted proudly up to the toy chest and let its contents spill to the floor. It was overflowing with fluffy balls. They were colored scarlet, and emerald green, and buttercup yellow, and cornflower blue; some had glitter and some had stripes, and some had flowers and some had mice and he hurled them playfully out at my cousin who gasped and giggled and finally wept.

"But my dearest Pansy," he said. "What's wrong?"

"They're just so beautiful," Pansy wept. " And I've never *seen* such incredible toys."

After the playroom, we toured the garden, Catsby announcing the names of the flowers and Pansy sniffing them, filling her nose with the heady catnip of raw perfume. I think she was drunk on it. Catsby whis-

21

pered, "I'd hoped to see you on April first. We had this party and Trout came by and I thought he'd bring you."

"He never does."

"Will you come on your own then? From now on?"

"Do you think it's proper?" she said. "I don't know. But I'd totally *love* you to come to Trout's. We only live about—"

"Yes, I know. I can see your house from the top of the pool. Would you like me to show you?"

We went to the pool where a man and a woman were sleeping soundly, if somewhat damply, on purple towels. We approached them carefully, sniffing their feet.

"Is that Zelda *Stardust*?" Pansy was awed.

"The very Zelda," Catsby agreed. "She and J.J.—" he flicked at the man— "have been—"

Pansy giggled, cutting him off. "I've heard they're an item. I heard it from Trout. It's completely thrilling, isn't it, Sam? I mean, *Zelda Stardust!*"

I wasn't thrilled. Zelda Stardust, who'd made her name as a famous model, was blonde and thin and predictably pretty and that was that.

J.J. Smythington, tall and dark, had a much more interesting look to his face and I circled around him, reading the time from his glittering Rolex: Ten after two.

"I'd better get going," I said. "But, look—if you wanted to stay here..."

My cousin laughed and said that of course she'd be leaving too. Catsby bowed to her. "Till tonight? The party's at seven, you know. The highlight— your roommate's reading— is set for eight, but first there's the drinking and then the eating. Skip your suppers," he

22

said to us both. "There'll be so much food here you'll barf for weeks."

5

As the afternoon faded into the evening, we watched the action on Catsby's lawn from the slanted terrace of Hunnicker's roof: The trucks from caterers, florists, bakers; the live musicians tuning guitars; an industrious army of sweaty workers setting up tables and canvas tents and scattering lights in the hovering trees as though it were Christmas. We watched and talked.

Pansy was fretful. "Tell me, Sam. Should I really be frightened? I mean, about Rex?"

I said, "Do you like him?"

She said, "I don't know. But I don't want him murdered."

"Of course you don't. But it's still very likely a practical joke. Besides—celebrities aren't killers, they're mostly suers."

"*Sewers?*" she said. "Like they're yicky holes full of yicky yuck?"

I started laughing. "You might have a point, but no,

what I meant was they'd take him to court and they'd sue him for lying."

She gave it some thought. "Like they sued the flounder, you mean? And the duck?"

I didn't answer. What could I say? And, more important, what could I do? If murder was brewing, I couldn't prevent it. I couldn't protect him, but Trout had a gun. And I hadn't been lying exactly, either. Angry celebrities reach for a lawyer, not for an ice pick.

I said, "Relax."

Hunnicker's sister appeared on the porch directly below us to offer us food and then, spotting us nesting, reported to Hunnicker, "No. I can see him. He's up on the roof and he's there with a girlfriend." Hunnicker laughed and said, "Fast worker," and that was that. His jangling sister went into the house and, after a while, we heard the sound of his wheezing Chevy chugging away.

At ten after seven the party began, the chattering ladies and serious men pouring into the garden like clotted ketsup, first a little and then a lot. Pansy breathlessly reeled off the names. There was Mort Yuckman and Tina Beige; Glorious Sternum and Barbara Strident; Steven Spellbinder, Martin Swann; there were both of the Briskets (Ethel and Harry), and later the Nazdacks along with the Sotts; there was Randy Muffin and Gordon Vidalia, Tizzie Swinelet and Harrison Twitt; there was Fluffy Pasternack (marmalade heiress), the brothers Tarpitz (from L.A.) and "there's Rex's editor, Marietta, the one in the purple with terrible hair? And look! there's J.J. and Zelda Stardust!"

I said, "There's lobster."

She said, "Let's go."

Catsby was waiting, right at the hedge that divided our properties, wearing a bow and a radiant, pitiful slobbering grin. Within several seconds, Pansy had joined him, off on another romantic tour, and I was alone in a crowd of strangers, brushing the ankles of famous legs, and looking for platters of low-hanging lox.

A tap on the shoulder caused me to turn, and there was Georgia, glowingly blonde and smelling of caviar, tiny beads of it still in her whiskers. "You having fun?"

I said, "Not exactly. How about you?"

"I'll show you how to," she answered slyly, and beckoned me merrily into the crowd with its sockless loafers and linen trousers and spiky sandals and frilly pastels. Her destination was off in a corner beside a fountain and under a tree where a platter of lobster sat on the lawn like a fish out of water. "It's Catsby's banquet," she whispered gaily. "He steals it slowly to leave for his friends."

I said, "And what else do you know about Catsby?"

Georgia toyed with a fishy claw. "Nobody knows," she said, "about Catsby. Or J.J. either." She licked at a shell. "I've heard some stories but none of them match."

"And what are the stories?"

"And why do you care?"

"It's simply my nature," I said, "to ask." I said nothing at all about Catsby's courting. None of my business and none of hers.

"I almost forgot you're a private detective. Speaking of which, did you find the book? Did it happen to mention a Mr. Rigby?"

"Who's Mr. Rigby?"

She shrugged. "A man."

"Well we didn't find it. We had to leave. Pansy came home with me. Just for tonight. I figured my job was protecting Pansy."

"You mean from Catsby?" Georgia was sly. I simply shrugged at her. Georgia laughed. "Very well, be silent," she said. "In any case, Catsby's coming."

And so he was. I could see him perfectly, ushering Pansy across the brilliant expanse of the lawn. The lights in the treetops were suddenly lit and the sound of the orchestra, playing softly the sounds of a sweeter and jazzier year, made them seem to be dancing.

"We saved you some lobster," Georgia was yelling.

But nobody cared. Catsby and Pansy were looking worried, and not about lobster.

"It's almost *nine*," Pansy said in a whisper that seemed to tingle with thrilling fear, "and the stupid reading was set for eight and he isn't here yet."

I scratched my ear.

"And his editor's screaming," Catsby announced. "She threatened to kill him for not showing up."

"Did anyone phone him?"

"He doesn't answer."

"Then let's get going," I said.

We left.

6

Rex's Lexus was still in the driveway. The house was silent, the windows, dark, but the door was open. A bad sign. I said to the women, "Wait on the porch," but they didn't want to. We padded in. The scene that hit us was bloody chaos. The white carpet was spattered red. The couch's cushions were thrown on the floor and a lamp was broken. Pansy said, "Oh," and turned in the doorway and went to the porch. Georgia said, "Heavens," and followed Pansy. I whispered to Catsby, "Look for a corpse." He went to the bedroom. I went to the kitchen where every cabinet seemed to be open and so was the oven. Whoever'd been in here— to look for the manuscript?—hadn't been lax. He'd looked in the oven! I went to the den.

It was worse than I'd figured, and more than a mess. The books and the photos had flown to the carpet. The chair was upended. The lamp was askew. I cat-footed carefully through the confusion— the spine-broken novels, the glass-shattered frames— and then leapt to the desktop. The telephone rang. A digital answerer barked, "Do your thing."

"My *THING...*" screaked the voice of an agitated crow, "is you get your tail over here in twenty-five minutes or—no, I won't strangle him, why would I strangle him? Never. I'll sue. Are you hearing that, Rexy? This is me, Marietta, and I'll sue you for every cent we paid for that book which, in case you've forgotten, is a cool half a mil. So you bring me that manuscript or bring me your cash." *Click!* Silence.

I glanced at the desk. The Royal typewriter stood as before. The halogen desk lamp was turned on its side but its bulb wasn't broken and its shade was intact. The drawers had been opened. The gun was now gone. So was the envelope that cradled the gun, the one with the picture of the globe sprouting wings. All that remained were a couple of pencils and the paper clip box that had once held the bullets but that no longer did. The rest of the drawers hadn't even been rifled. They held what they'd held: The Ham phonebook, the high school yearbook, the spiral notebooks, the odds and ends.

Catsby was nosing around in the living room, checking the hiding place under the couch.

"I take it there's nothing?"

"Nothing so far." He wriggled his head out and shook off some dust. "The bedroom's been ransacked, but that's about it. Nobody's body," he added, "or blood. Shall I tell the ladies...?"

I nodded yes. He went out through the door again, onto the porch, and I looked at the living room, looking for clues.

The blood on the carpet was next to the hallway

that led to the bedroom. In front of the clock. I looked at the clock which was smashed by a bullet; the bullet had stopped it at twenty to six. Another bullet had entered the wall and I looked for the angle the bullets had taken. They seemed to have come from the door of the den.

From somewhere behind me, Pansy was weeping. I turned and faced her. "Try to be calm. The worst thing we know is the manuscript's missing and so is your roommate."

"Who's probably dead."

"We aren't sure of that, Pansy darling." I looked at the clock and the hole in the wall and the blood on the carpet. I pointed them out. "All we're sure of, at least so far, is that shots were fired—probably three—and they must've been fired at twenty to six."

"Why *three*?" Catsby puzzled. "There's one in the clockface and one in the wall."

"And blood on the carpet."

"So?" he said

"So? Two of the bullets missed but the other one didn't."

"Then Rex has been wounded," he said, "at the least."

"We're not sure of that either. For all we can say now, he could have been the shooter instead of the victim. Like somebody broke in and he grabbed his own gun."

Pansy looked doubtful but said, "I suppose."

"That's all we can do now," I said. "Suppose." I could also suppose it the other way around. That Trout had walked in on the burgling burglar who'd brought his own pistol and shot from the den. There was no use supposing. "Eventually," I said, "the police will come out here —"

"You think they'll come out here?" She frowned at me. "Why?"

"Because," I said firmly, "Marietta's gonna call them. Give it less than half an hour, she'll be barreling through the door. In the meanwhile—" I started— "by the way, where's Georgia?"

Pansy sniffled. "Still on the porch. She said the blood makes her barfy."

I looked at the drying blood. There wasn't a whole lot of it, all things considered. A couple of stains about nine inches round and a couple of splatterings that trailed off the rug. "Let's see where it splatters to." I gestured to Catsby. "You want to play detective?" He eagerly came along.

We followed the drip-drip trail of the droplets to the edge of the back hallway that led to the back yard. "Hold on," I said suddenly. "Wait. Something's wrong." I hesitated. Yes! There'd been a rug here before. I remembered how this morning, when I'd plunged through the cat-door, that I'd landed— quite comfortably, in fact— on a rug. But now there was only the impression of a rug, its outline distinguished by an oval absence of dust. On the other side of the oval—more drippings and more dust.

"Let's get going," I said to Catsby.

"Where to?" he said.

"Out."

We went out through the cat-door and into the yellow night. The moon had grown gaudier. The air smelled of salt. The dirt on the rear pathway had the faintest odor of Trout.

31

"What are we looking for?" Catsby halted.

"We're looking for *that*." I was pointing down. There were several shoe prints—possibly sneakers— sharply defined on the face of the ground. A size eleven, I reckoned quickly. Their rubber soles had the pattern of stars. Next to the star-prints, a splatter of blood and then definite drag marks eroded the path—as though something of weight had been dragged through the dirt. We followed the trail till it veered from the pathway and then disappeared into trampled-on grass, and I looked up ahead to see where it was leading. Down to the water. Down to the bay. And there, once again, there was something different. I stopped and waited. The boat was gone! I stared at the shore line and after a while I nodded my head and concluded, "So."

"This is rather maddening," Catsby muttered. He peered at the distance and angled his head. "I see nothing out there."

I said, "I know." I explained it to Catsby: It looked as though someone had dragged a body, wrapped in a rug, and taken it off in the missing rowboat.

"You mean and dumped it?"

I said, "In the bay. But that's how it *looks*," I said, leaving hedge room. "It's not necessarily—"

"Still. I'm convinced."

"Better keep it from Pansy." I glanced at the house. "You think you could manage to stay here a while? To report what happens? I mean, with the cops?"

"Shall I gather you're going?"

"To look for a witness." I thought about Virgil and Virgil's tree. He might have been watching. "Take care of our girl."

He nodded grimly and turned to the path— a man with a mission, a knight with a quest and a beautiful damsel to save from distress. He was slightly comic and deeply touching. I watched him leaving and turned to go.

Georgia, as promised, was still on the porch at the front of the cottage. I said, "You okay?"

"Not exactly really."

"I'm going *that* way—" I pointed hazily out at the woods— "to look for a witness. You want to come?"

"Absolutely never. I'm going home. But just by the way, if you're after a witness, you might want to look for the roving Tom. He might have come back here, you know, for supper, and seen what happened."

"And where would he be?"

"He'd be with his girlfriend, I guess."

"And where—"

"I haven't the foggiest," Georgia said. "But you're the detective."

I said, "Uh-huh."

7

The woods were moonlit which made them eerie. The sounds of night critters hummed in the air. I became a night critter, yowling "Virgil?" And after a while he responded, "Yo."

I zipped to his tree house—zippety-zap— but after I got there, the best I could do was to sit there in agony, chasing my breath. I couldn't catch it. I gulped the view. The starlit sky was indifferently brilliant; the stone-faced moon was a glittering eye. And somewhere below me, the twin of the moon, in a moment of merriment, danced on the bay, turning the bay, in the darkening distance, into a saucer of liquid light.

Virgil examined me. "Bad as you look?"

I glanced at him somberly. "How do I look?"

"Like an orphan flea on a hamster's butt."

"Does that have any meaning?"

"It means you look low. What's the matter there, Slicker? You might as well say."

I told him the matter.

He waggled his head. "Idiot people," he muttered sadly. "Better to mix with 'em only for food. You wanted to bunk in my treetop, Slicker, you're thoroughly welcome to stay the night."

"I'd like to do that," I said, and meant it, "except I figure I'm on the case. I was kind of hoping to find a witness."

"You mean a witness that saw the shooting?"

"Or else a witness that heard the shots?"

"Well now that you mention it," Virgil allowed, "I heard a few bangers from earlier on. I thought it's them crackers they use in July."

"So how many bangers?" I offered a guess. "Three in a row of them? Bang-bang-bang?"

"Nope," he said carefully. "Bang and bang. There was only the two of em. Bang and bang. It likened to woke me."

"You'd fallen asleep?"

He looked at me balefully. "That's what I said."

"How long were you sleeping?"

"From after you left."

"So you didn't see anyone go to the house. How about later? Did anyone leave?"

"'Bout an hour some later, I did see a bike. Come along up Featherstone, zips to the left. Couldn't say where it come from, it could've been Trout's."

"Did you see who was on it?"

"I 'spose in a way. Didn't know I'd be tested on what-all I seed or I'd tooken some notes on it. Best I could say, it was rid by a human. Whoever it was, it got one of them hoodies. The hoodie was up so it could've been anyone, boy type or girl. I could tell you the bike, though. It's taxi yellow. So why're you askin'? You

35

sound like a cop."

"I'm a private detective."

"You pullin' my tail?"

"Look at me, Virgil, and look at your tail."

He looked at me slowly and looked at his tail. "Well, ain't that a kicker. A private eye! Which one of 'ems private?"

"The left one," I said and winked at him broadly.

Virgil guffawed. "What else can I tell you?"

I gave it some thought. He'd possibly slept through the first of the shots so I asked him instead "Could you tell me the time? When you heard those bangers—the two or the three—"

Without hesitation, he said, "It was two."

" 'Two' meaning bangers," I said. "Okay. I'll give you the number, I asked you—"

"The time. You asked me the *time*, and I said it was two."

I squinted dumbly.

He said, "O'clock."

"You mean two o'clock...*in the afternoon?*"

"You gettin' ditzy there, fella? Yeah. There was two of them bangers at two o'clock."

"Are you sure of that, Virgil? I mean, of the time?"

He looked at me darkly.

I looked at the sky. "I was figuring maybe..." I started.

"*What?*"

"Well...*maybe*..." I muttered, "*maybe* you slept longer than you thought."

"Nope. I can always think longer'n I sleep. I can think about seven hours, I can sleep about maybe three."

36

I decided to let it go. The grandfather clock, an objective witness, was stopped by a bullet at twenty to six and it hadn't been napping. Virgil's opinion was just an opinion, it wasn't a fact, but Virgil was steady and canny and wise so my mind remained open, if only an inch.

I took a chance with another angle. "How about later?" I said. "You also happen to be here at twenty to six?"

"Just so happened," he said. "Yup. I come directly after I et. It was nice and quiet, 'cept for the birds, and the sun was yonder." He pointed west, where the sun would have settled before it would set.

"So the hooded biker went off to the west." I squinted down through the leafy distance, down at the curve of the moonlit road which traveled from Pansy's house, on the right, and ended, left, in a wall of trees. "So where was he going? What's at the left?"

"Potato patches is mostly it. Coupla farms that's owned by the locals. After that, there's a bunch of railroad tracks and then you're in West Ham."

"Any suspects in West Ham? Someone who might've been gunning for Trout?"

"You're lookin for gossip," he said, "go to Nosey. Nosey knows everything nobody knows. He works at the paper."

"The *Ham Herald* ?"

"It's over the tracks there in West Ham. Corner of Main Street. You can't miss it."

"One other question," I said. "Tom. You know where I'd find him?"

"I'd reckon at Flo's. And afore you ask me, she lives at the docks."

"And the docks would be—"

"Corner of Blueberry Hill. When you get to the *Herald,* you turn to the left. Blue wooden cottage."

I said, "At the docks?"

"That's what I told you." He waggled his head. "The boy doesn't listen," he said to the moon. "You tell him the first time, he asks you again."

"I'll try to do better," I said.

He laughed.

8

Crouching sullenly under an overpass, the railroad tracks drew a straight, cold, and oddly symbolic line between the place where the living was easy and the place where the living was hard. Glancing back at the leafy farmland, glancing up at the lighted hills, I crossed the line into deepening darkness. There was nothing and no one around. A halogen street lamp glared at the pit of a dirt-covered lot with a chain-metal fence and a rattling sign that said *Auto Repairs*. Right underneath it, in smaller letters, it offered the rest of the deal: *And Parts*. Most of the *Parts* appeared to be tires. A dozen rows of them, stacked as neatly as licorice Lifesavers, littered the lot and a couple of field mice raced on the rims. They heard me coming and dove through the hole.

Across the street from the rodent racetrack, a giant billboard looked at the tracks through the spectacled eyes of a white-coated man whose paternal expression was cheerful and kindly but not without subtle sugges-

tions of guile. The headline surrounding him offered a
rhyme:

FEELING ILL?

NEED A PILL?

DR. HERMAN (THE GERM MAN) JECKYLBURG

AT 70 BLUEBERRY HILL

I trotted past him and headed west. When I'm feeling ill, I go under the bookshelf and wait till it's over;
it works like a charm, and I've never been hassled
for bookshelf insurance or Medicat payments or bills
from the vet. Of course I've been lucky and "lucky"
can change. I scanned the horizon for changes of luck:
wandering schnauzers, mischievous thugs. Nothing and
no one. I doubled my speed. After a while, in the midst
of the nothing, the street grew brighter and sprouted
stores. *Davey's Diner. Hannigan's Hardware. Beads
'n' Baubles. Dishes 'n' Things.* I was getting closer to
civilization— the home of silly expensive *Things*— and
further from basics like hardware and food. When I got
to the corner, as Virgil'd promised, I found the *Herald*,
housed by itself in a modest townhouse of weathered
brick. A ground floor window, barred against burglars,
was happily open. A lamp was on. I could see its glow in
the inner distance. I took the window and slithered in.

The room I entered was long and narrow. Stacks
of newspapers climbing the walls held the dusty odor
of winter scandals and spring engagements and Final
Sales. A couple of desks, stretching into the distance,
were cluttered with papers and boxes and phones and
with ancient computers that glowed in the dark. From
the back of the press room (if that's what it was), an
angular cat sitting under a desk lamp, pounding an
iMac and, pausing to sneeze, looked up from his labors

40

and said, "Ah hah! Private detective. Hot on the case."

"I beg your pardon?" I paused on the sill.

"According to sources who chose to be nameless, she said you'd be coming."

I nodded. "She. I expect that's Georgia?"

"I couldn't say."

I leapt from the window and crossed to his desk. From closer up, he looked sharp and snappy— a bony bundle of black and white with a fur tuxedo and hungry eyes. He appraised me cooly. "You're Sam The Cat."

"And you must be Nosey."

He nodded twice. "Nosey by nature and Nosey by name."

"What else did she tell you? I mean, your source."

He flicked a grin at me. "Trout cooked. Apparent victim of foul play."

"You put that nicely."

"Nicely's my job."

"You mean you're a writer."

"Writing's for chumps. I'm the overnight editor. See, what I do is I edit their copy when everyone's gone. Sometimes they notice it, sometimes they don't."

"But you make it better."

"You bet your tail."

"Speaking of betting," I said, "I bet there've been plenty of bets about who's in the book."

"You mean Rex's 'novel'?" Yeah. There's a pool. Six-hundred bucks if you hit the trifecta."

"Meaning the first three names in the book. What are the favorites?"

"Here at the paper? The hottest stories we never told. Couldn't get the goods on em. Plenty of rumors but, coming down to it, not any facts."

"So you didn't publish."

"Not without proof."

"But Trout could publish."

"Sure. It's a 'novel.'" Nosey looked up at me, cackling aloud.

"So what are the stories?"

"First make a deal. If you find the killer, I get the exclusive."

"You get the exclusive. So what are the tales?"

"Wall Street Biggie in Boomtown Bust. Canary Questioned in Housebreak Horror, Artful Arson or—"

"Hold it a second. Those are the headlines. Give me the meat."

"The Wall Street biggie is Marlon Maykout. Rumor has it he's selling stocks that he isn't selling, you get what I mean. He's selling shares of imagination. Nobody's proved it but that's what they think."

"And the questioned canary?"

"Is Mona Fragg. Nightclub singer who married smart and then shot her husband, a billionaire, who she thought was a burglar. Or that's what she said."

"And she wasn't convicted?"

"There wasn't a trial. Her sister's husband, the county sheriff, ruled it a 'terribly tragic mistake.'"

"So she's gotten away with it."

"Yep. Till now."

"That'd give her a motive."

"For icing Trout? But they all got motives. Next on the list would be 'Artful Arson Or Flukey Fire?' and 'More Mings Missing from Mandelbaum Manse.'" He looked at me sheepishly. "Sorry. Forgot. The Mings in question are Ming vases. Very expensive. Very antique. Boosted by Tabatha 'Tippi' Tapp—"

42

"From a Mr. Mandelbaum?"

"Nah. From herself. To collect the insurance. The Mandelbaum mansion was where she was living. Her and her cat and her hideous husband. They bought the estate."

"And she's gotten away with it."

"Yep. Till now."

"And the artful arson...?"

"Is Harold Rigby. Burned his office. Right to the ground."

"To collect the insurance?"

"To burn his records. He skipped his taxes. For twenty years. The feds caught on and they sent him a summons but, oopsy-doopsy." He cackled again.

"This is some little city you got here, Nosey."

"You think it's different from any place else?"

I thought it over and shook my head. It wasn't different, except for richer. Small-time chiselers were eating the map. My brilliant country was losing its vision, its old-fashioned virtues of working hard and behaving nicely and playing fair. We were turning harder and turning soft. We were snarky anglers, loaded with bluster and whiny whimpers of "me, me, me." I believe devoutly, of course, in the "me"— in the sovereign soul that pursues its happiness, bets on its chances, and takes its lumps. But the modern "me" was a cheating cardsharp— a rotten loser, a sniveling Self.

"We were up to four," I announced. "There are six."

Nosey was pacing the length of the desk. "The others are longshots." He turned with a shrug. "J.J. Smythington—"

"J.J.? Why?"

"I couldn't be certain. Nobody knows. But he

comes out of nowhere and flashes cash. So how did he make it?"

"How do you think?"

"One story goes he's a gambler from Vegas. One story goes he's a hitman from Chi."

"Did anyone ask him?"

"Everyone asks him. Twelve different answers. He lies like a rug."

"So he's hiding a secret and Trout could've found it." I nodded slowly. "And who's number six?"

"My personal guess would be Zelda Stardust. Actually, nobody thinks it but me. But I happen to know from anonymous sources that Trout had a thing for her."

" 'Thing' meaning...?"

"Thing. Crush. Fancies. Unbelievably high hopes. I heard he discovered her. Found her in Starbucks whipping up lattes in Kalamazoo. Introduced her to bigshots. Built her career. But it wasn't romantic. At least not for her."

"And you think she's got secrets?"

"Everyone has."

I had to agree with him—everyone has. There's always something we've done that's nasty or less than honest or more than wrong, and we all try to bury it deep in our heads and hope no one discovers it. Not even us.

I glanced for a moment at Nosey's computer. An empty e-mail blank filled the screen and the cursor was winking. I got an idea. "Do you mind if I use it before I forget?"

"Forget how to use it?"

"Forget what you said. The names and the secrets."

44

He nodded, "Go on," and I settled beside him and typed what he'd told.

Harold Rigby	Burned building
Tippi Tapp	Stole Mings
Mona Fragg	Shot husband
Zelda Stardust	

What had she done? I hadn't a clue because neither did Nosey which left me to settle for:

	Did things.
Catsby's roommate	Total phony
Marlon Maykout	Phony stocks
This could either be	Baloney
Or, with luck,	It might be lox.

"Kill the end of it," Nosey grumbled. "Too many words and it doesn't make sense."

"But it does to *me*." I explained to Nosey how I'm paid for a case in lox, so lox, symbolically, means success. "And aside from that," I declared, "it rhymes. And when anything rhymes, I remember it better." I stared at my handiwork, trying to burn its important contents into my head. Could I really remember it, rhyming or not? And then it hit me. Hunnicker'd shlepped his reliable laptop out to the Hams and, even now, it was up on his dresser...

I filled in the subject— *Tricks of the Six*— typed my address in and pounded SEND.

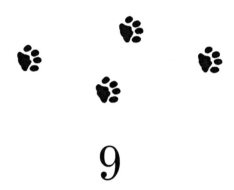

9

Virgil'd told me to make a left when I left the *Herald* to look for the docks, so I hung a left and proceeded leftward, sniffing for water and looking for ships. The sidewalk ahead of me, chilling my paws, was as empty and dark as a Doberman's head, though a pale mist of light sifted out from a building whose darkened awning said *Ham Hotel*.

I skirted it quickly and raced up the block. The hamlet of Ham was asleep for the night. Its elegant stores, with their baubles and beach hats, were totally silent; their windows were dark, their mannequins, frozen like Sleeping Beauties, attentively waiting the kiss of the sun.

I kept on moving, compelled by those humorless plastic faces, those out-of-it eyes, those make-believe dream girls with make-believe dreams, till I got to a sign that said *Blueberry Hill*. According to Virgil, the docks —and Flo's, where Tom would be hiding— were somewhere about, so I followed the street sign and tackled the hill.

The street ran upward, fronted by houses—some of them grayish and some of them white, and some of them lighted by lights in the windows and some of them lighted by lights on the porch. I could see a house number once in a while (127...124) but addresses were meaningless. "Blue wooden cottage" was all Virgil'd told me. That, and "the docks."

I heard some yapping and froze on the spot. I turned my head slowly and caught a Chihuahua, hurling its pitiful frame at a fence that it couldn't get over and couldn't get through. I tossed it a growl on the general order of "Wee little pups are my favorite lunch," and it suddenly whimpered and ran like a rat.

I continued climbing, pursuing the promise of possibly sometime encountering docks, when I noticed a house that was hung on the hilltop and seemed, in the moonlight, decidedly blue.

I got to it quickly and hit my own head. A sign at the curbside proclaimed it the office of one Dr. Herman (The Germ Man) Jeckylburg, which sat —as it said in his billboard ad— at 70 Blueberry Hill.

"She lives at the *Doc's!*" I exclaimed it aloud. "He didn't say *docks*, what he said was *Doc's!*"

"Would you button your yapper?" I turned and looked up at a chocolate shorthair who sat on the sill of a half-open window ahead in the house. "Would you stifle the riot? My friend is asleep."

"I apologize deeply," I said, "but I tend to get overexcited whenever I'm dumb." I looked him over. "You wouldn't be Tom?"

"I certainly wouldn't," he said. "If I'd had any say in the matter, I would have been Rick. Or maybe

47

Tobias. Or possibly Steve. I used to be Teddy and once I was Chip— on account of the chocolate— and then I was Scat. For a couple of winters, in fact, I was Scat. Like I'd come around people, they'd yell at me 'Scat!' "

"The fate of the drifter," I offered.

"Tell me."

I didn't have to. We both knew the tale. People adopt you and then they desert you and then you're unhappy and then you don't care. I could tell that he didn't. The cat before me was perfectly, properly, self-possessed and as free as a tiger.

"But now you're a Tom?"

He shrugged his indifference and rattled his tail. "When the idiots name you," he said, "you get stuck. You're whatever they name you. The same with their kids. There's a family in Linden, their last name is Soar and they named their kid Dinah. The kid oughta sue." He looked at me flatly. "So what about you?"

"I'm a private detective," I said, "and I'm Sam and I figure it suits me. I'm here on a case. Could I ask you some questions?"

He narrowed his eyes. "Is the case about murder?"

I nodded. "You know."

He nodded agreement. "We'll take it inside."

I leapt to the window and followed him in.

The room I got into was spare and dark. There were raggedy chairs that appeared to be coughed on or possibly puked on or maybe just old. A couple of tables with dull magazines. A receptionist's setup—a wooden counter that hid the confusion that rode on the desk, and on top of the counter, arranged in a comma, an orange enchantress mewed in her sleep.

Tom raised his paw with the sound of a "Shussh"

and then silently gestured me into an office that wasn't much grander than where we'd just been. A wooden desk and a couple of chairs and a gleaming certificate nailed to the wall:

Be It Known That
Herman Jeckylburg, MD
Is licensed to practice Medicine
In the State of New York

Tom took his place on the top of the blotter; I settled uncomfortably onto the chair. "So," I said levelly, "what do you know and how do you know it?"

He narrowed his eyes. "Who are you working for?"

"Pansy's my cousin."

"Oh." He was silent and stared at his feet. "I can really explain this. I mean about Flo and the—"

"Save it for later," I said. "Get to Trout."

He paced on the desktop and built me a shrug. "I got home about five," he said. "Dinner's at five but my platter was empty and so was the house. The place had been ransacked. Blood on the floor and some—"

"Hold it a second," I said, "this was *five*?"

"Make it 4:47," he said, "if you care. The 4:30 train whistled in from Manhattan, I headed for chicken."

I stared at the wall. "And the house was ransacked. And Rexy was gone."

"I figured a goner." Tom shook his head. "He'd been asking for trouble and trouble arrived."

"Must've gotten there early." I thought of the clock that was notably shattered at twenty to six and of Virgil's insisting the shots were at two. "And what else did you notice?"

"I didn't. I left. I went out to find Pansy."

I said, "She's with me.— Any guesses whodunit?"

"Like half of the town."

"Would your guess include Zelda?'

"Witorski?"

"Stardust."

"Witorski, Stardust. Same either way. It was Rex named her Stardust. Brought her to Ham from some middle-west boondocks a few summers back. Introduced her to big shots to boost her career. Introduced her to J.J. and, man, that was that." He paused and looked thoughtful. "Heck, I suppose if you're chasing for motives, it's Rex'd kill *her*."

"You mean...out of jealousy?"

"Nah. Out of pride. When you get to the heart of it, Trout's about Trout. The people he knows are just food for his column. And food for his ego."

"And food for his book.—Did you happen to read the thing?"

"Nope."

"Ever see it?"

"I once saw a box with its title on top. Flo could've killed me for not peeking in but it didn't—"

"Occur to him. Isn't that rich?" The voice from the doorway was pleasantly shrill. The orange siren was rolling her eyes as she entered the office and said, "Mr. Class," but she said it good-humoredly, even with pride. Close up she was plainer than what she'd appeared. Her face was forthright, without any grace, and one of her eyeballs was slightly askew, but her eyes were merry and brimming with life. "We'd have solved the whole murder," she said, "if he'd looked."

"So he told you what happened," I said.

"Well of course. It was such a coincidence. Trout

50

being here on the day he was murdered. Just hours before."

"Trout being *here?*" I was still being stupid. He'd been to the doctor; that much I knew. But to Herman The Germ Man? It didn't compute.

"As a first-time patient," she said with a shrug. "He came at eleven."

"And left...?"

"Around noon. I happen to know since he left with the doctor."

"They left together?"

She nodded yes.

"And when, after that, did the doctor return?"

"He didn't ever," she said. "He doesn't. Not on the weekends. It's nine till noon and then he goes fishing or something. Oh! But Mr. Trout came back. For his glasses. Ten minutes later, he knocks on the door. Mrs. Rolf, the receptionist, lets him back in. 'I've forgotten my sunglasses,' says Mr. Trout and he goes to the room where the patients lie down and comes out with his glasses and that was the end."

I considered it slowly. The timing was right. It was probably one when he'd entered his driveway and Pansy and I had gone scampering out. "And how did he look to you. Sickish? Ill?"

"I thought he looked normal. Except that he happened to smell like a sweat bomb," she added. "*Pyew!* And I think Dr. J must've thought the same thing. What I mean is he said to him— right in the waiting room— 'Call me next week for results of your tests but you want my opinion, I'd say that you're fine. Just take that prescription and try to relax.'"

So Trout had been "fine" but he'd rushed to a doctor.

51

A brand new doctor, demanding "tests." Well, okay. He was probably nervous. Someone who's nervous can work up a sweat and can feel like he's dying, or fear that he will. And Trout had some reasons to fear that he might.

Flo said politely, "Can *I* ask a question?"

I turned and looked up at her. "Sure you can. Shoot."

"Can I ask what your name is? I'm blabbering on, and I don't even know who I'm blabbering *to*."

I started to answer but Tom interrupted, supplying my name and the gist of my job though he notably skipped my relation to Pansy.

"A real life detective?" she said. "Heaven's sake! Would you stay for a biscuit?"

"She made them herself," Tom announced with approval.

She waggled her head. "Well, I didn't exactly," she said, looking down, "but I made them come out of the bag to the floor and they're mighty delicious and good for the teeth."

I told her politely I had to move on but I thanked her sincerely for all her trouble and fine information and offer of food.

Tom said abruptly, "I'll see you out," and before I could tell him he didn't have to, he started parading me back to the sill. We cleared the window and hit the lawn and, still saying nothing, he led to the street. He stopped at the curb and said, "Look— about Pansy—"

"It's none of my business," I said. "None at all. If you want to come see her..." I gave my address, and he said he'd be over as soon as he could.

"But I wanted to tell you that Flo— Flo and I are

just—well, Flo and I are just excellent friends. We have interests in common. Like hunting and fishing and sort of just racing around   on the lawn and Pansy's so... ladylike and so...clean and so wonderfully—"

"Lazy," I added.

He laughed. "But so beautifully lazy," he said with a grin. "I barely deserve her. A bum like me."

"Love can be funny," I said.

"It can." He stood for a moment, lit by the moonlight and seemingly saddened by something inside. Then he turned slowly and went to the house.

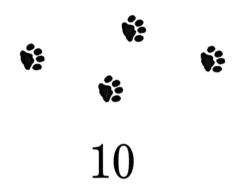

10

It was screamingly yellow, all right. The bike that was suddenly parked at the Ham Hotel was as brilliantly yellow as yellow can get. It was egg yolk yellow, daffodil yellow, sunflower yellow, lemon meringue.

I circled around it and sniffed at its seat. The faint aroma of human being had practically faded; the seat was cold. It hadn't been ridden for several hours. Could I really have missed it before when I'd passed? I probably could have. I vaguely remembered I'd focussed my eyes on the glorious dolls. I circled again and looked under its seat. A peeling sticker said, *Mike's Bikes, Rent by the hour/ Rent by the week/ Willington Avenue, Stag Harbor*. It didn't help me. I moved to the street.

The Ham Hotel was a red brick building with white wooden shutters, a white wooden door, and a forest green awning that fronted a porch. Three stories high, it was weathered and cozy and seemed to belong to that part of the past where the people were smaller, the future was bigger, and cats in the sycamores squinted at France. A plaque on the cornerstone seemed to confirm it: *Washington Slept Here*, it said on the brass, *Building Erected in 1712.*

I leapt to the edge of a checker-paned window and angled my head in and squinted around. The lobby was cheerful and mostly antique. Wood-panelled walls and a flower-strewn carpet. A couple of club chairs in cornflower blue and a couple of benches in cream-colored silk. Away at the left was a cherrywood counter behind which a night clerk was texting the news ("I'm alone in the lobby") to all of his friends, and then, facing the windows, a door to *The Lounge*. From somewhere behind it, the buzz of a crowd and the beat of a samba was blasting the air.

I smelled the Angora before I could see him. And then I saw him, arranged in a chair where, disguised as a pillow, he snored in his sleep. He was white and silver and glowingly young and I didn't like him, which wasn't fair, but then, to my sorrow, I'm frequently not. I streaked through the lobby and plopped to the chair. A brilliantly green and incurious eye opened up for a second and instantly shut. "How dare you disturb me," he said, "I'm asleep."

"Well...not exactly," I argued. "You were, but my plopping awakened you."

"Technically true. But I'm right now pretending your plop never happened."

"And how's that been going?"

He curled in a ball, resuming the pose of a ermine pillow, his flat little face in the crook of his tail.

"Look," I said softly, "it's very important. Assuming you work here, I wanted to—"

"Work??" He jerked himself upright and gave me a glare. "Do I *look* like I'm working?" He thumped with his tail. "Are you even suggesting I look like I *work*?"

The way he said "work" was the way someone sane would say "poop on the carpet" or "fetch like a dog."

"I'm the owner," he snooted. "I own the hotel. My godfather left me the place in his will. I own the whole mansion and everything in it. And everyone in it," he said, "works for *me*. Nobody shoos me or tells me to scat. I can shed where I want to and puke where I will. I could puke in the lobby, you know what they'd do? They'd go, 'Poor little Pookie' and clean up the mess."

"So your name would be *Pookie*," I sneered.

"It would. It's a name of distinction," he said with a glare. "And you mind your manners,"

I said, "I don't. I don't happen to mind them the teeniest bit. I think they're delightful, in fact. But of course, if you happen to mind them, I'll put them away."

"And you think you're funny," he said. "You apparently think it's amusing to ruin my sleep."

"I'm a private detective," I said, "on a case. And I haven't got time to keep batting the breeze. There's a big yellow bike at the side of your porch. Do you know who owns it?"

"And what if I did?"

"Well, you could tell me," I tried, "and I'd leave."

He thought it over. "Before you left, would you tell me I'm pretty and sing me a song? I never get sung to since god-papa died."

I suddenly softened. The arrogant "owner," in spite of his bragging, was lonely and lost and the cowering of servants was nothing like love.

"You got it," I promised.

"It's Mr. McGee's."

"And Mr. McGee would be—"

"Nobody much. He arrived last Thursday and booked for a week. He said he's a salesman and might go away, that he might go away for an overnight trip but he paid for his lodgings a week in advance."

"So he's here until Wednesday."

"I guess. In a way. He left here at four-ish and got on the bus and he left with his luggage but said he'd be back."

"And where did he go to?"

The teenager shrugged. "Wherever the bus goes. It ends in New York, but it stops other places." He yawned. "Are we through?"

"In a couple of seconds. This Mr. McGee— can you say what he looks like?"

"He's medium tall and a little bit paunchy. His hair would be black but, you want my opinion, it isn't his hair."

"And what was he wearing today when he left?"

"A cream-colored suit and a yellowish tie."

"Did you see him before in some jeans and a hoodie?"

"Indeed," Pookie nodded. "Today around three. He chained up his bike and then entered the lobby. And then, like I told you, he left around four."

"You've been wonderfully helpful," I said. "And you're pretty. I honestly mean it. You totally are."

"Am I really and truly?"

I patted his head. "Oh my poor little Pookie," I muttered sincerely, and sang him a chorus of *Heartbreak Hotel*.

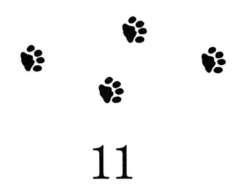

11

The glittering eyeballs of Dr. Jeckylburg seemed to be watching me crossing the tracks. I squinted back at him, high on his billboard, above the confusions of life on the ground. Could he see to the future? Unravel the past? Could he fathom the reasons for living and dying or cure the uncertainties cramping the soul? I silently asked him in earnest wonder. His only answer was:

NEED A PILL?

I bounded quickly across the potato field, hanging a left onto Featherstone Road where I passed a few houses of various sizes, but all of them silent and sleepily dark. I kept to the shoulder, picking my way among dirt-covered pebbles and tough little weeds, and sniffing the air for the scent of coyote. I didn't smell one. I plodded on. Once in a while, a car hurtled past me, projecting a ribbon of light on the road and then roaring away, leaving scarier silence. A chorus of crickets chirred in the distance. An owl hooted. A bullfrog burped. If this was the country, I wanted the city, where avenues tingled with neon and noise and the nights weren't lonely, and pretty potatoes were sitting in gravy instead of in fields.

I stopped and recovered at Pansy's mailbox. The Japanese lantern was still on the tree but it dangled there darkly — a busted illusion, a moon without magic, a lamp without light. I waited in search of illumination. I needed a moment to know what I'd learned. Or maybe a moment to learn what I knew.

Start with the basics:

Trout was missing. Certainly missing. Potentially dead.

Shots had been fired. Virgil had heard them. I'd looked at the bullets. I'd looked at the clock. The clock had been shattered at twenty to six. But whatever was done here was done before five because Tom had come back here at just before five and then Virgil had told me the shots were at two. I began to believe him. At least on the time though I still had a hunch he'd miscounted the shots. I was thinking it over. I pictured the clock. Had it possibly stopped before anyone shot it? Like maybe this morning? Or maybe last night? The twenty-to-sixes came twice in a day and it might have been one of them. Maybe. Or not. So hold that for later. What else did I know?

There were seven suspects. Six of the locals whose names I'd forgotten and Mr. McGee, the Mysterious Stranger. Virgil had seen him at just about threeish on Featherstone Road though he might or might not have been coming from Trout's. But where did that get me and what did it mean? He didn't live here. He'd stayed at the Ham. He'd even rented his infamous bike. It wasn't a crime to be biking at threeish or even to borrow some bad-looking hair which, as Pookie described it, was phony and black. If bad-looking rugs were a cause for suspicion, a quarter of Congress would now be in jail. I began to conclude he was just a distraction. Lacking a motive, he wasn't a clue, he was just a coincidence leading to zip. I left him behind me and moved to the house.

The first thing I saw was the yellow police tape that ran from the posts at the sides of the porch and then criss-crossed the doorway:

ATTENTION! CRIME SCENE.
DO NOT ENTER. DO NOT CROSS.

I trotted around to the rear cat door and plunked myself noisily into house. "Catsby?" I hollered.

"Indeed. We're in here."

I followed his voice into Rex's workroom where Catsby and Pansy were sprawled on the desk in a lamp-lighted clutter of spiral notebooks— the same spiral notebooks I'd seen in the drawer. A couple were open and Pansy, exhausted, was sweetly asleep at the edge of a page.

I jumped to the desktop and blinked in the light. "So what did the cops say?" I whispered to Catsby.

"Exactly what you did." He eyed me with awe. "I mean word for word of it. Right down the line. Right to the part about rolled in the carpet and stuck on the rowboat and dumped in the bay."

"Including the part about twenty to six?"

He nodded, smiling.

I muttered, "Oy."

"You'll forgive me," he blurted. "Would that have been Swedish?"

"Would what have been Swedish?"

"It sounded like Oy."

I said, "It's New Yorkish. It means...it means... Oy. Which is loosely translated as sort of Oh boy if you said the Oh boy with your eyes rolled to heaven and—"

Catsby just stared at me, head to the side.

"It *means*," I said, sighing, "the shots were at two." I explained how I knew it and Catsby said, "Oy."

Pansy awakened and yawned in my face with those taunting aromas of tuna and sleep.

"Oh dear," she said, stretching, "I must have gone off. Did he tell the whole story?"

"Of what?"

"Of the cops?"

I nodded. "I think so."

She said, "Are you sure? Like the part about how they don't know who's the victim and how they won't know till they check out the blood?"

"I suppose they took samples."

"They scraped the whole rug."

"And *then*," Catsby added, "they copied the footprints. The ones on the pathway? The ones with the stars?"

I remembered the footprints and pictured the stars.

"And *then*—" Pansy giggled— "well, they really got ridiculous. They said how tomorrow they'd be *dragging the bay!* Now is that major moron? I mean, drag it where? I mean, where would they put it? It's not like there's room. And, aside from all that, it's gi*nor*mously heavy."

I started to laugh, although it wasn't why she thought, and then gently explained about dragging a bay. Dragging a bay means you're searching its bottom. "It's done with a net—called a dragnet," I said. "And you drop it from a boat and you drag it through the bay. What you're looking for," I said, "would be something that would sink. Like a boat. Or a gun."

"Or a body," Catsby said, which he instantly regretted.

Pansy looked alarmed again. "Oh," she said. "*Oh*."

For a moment we were silent, the three of us sitting in the clutter on the desk in the harsh glare of lamplight. I looked around the room. The stuff that was scattered on the floor was still scattered— the books and the pictures lay in jumbles as before. As much to change the subject as to get the information, I asked about who had come around to call the cops.

"The call," Pansy said, "came from Marietta Snidely."

"Except," Catsby added, "Marietta wasn't first. Before she came knocking, there was— what's the fellow's name?"

"Marlon Maykout," Pansy said. "Marlon Maykout came first. I just happen to know his name because once, a long time ago, Rex bought his socks and he lost a lot of money. I believe they were broken. Though however you'd break a sock is beyond me by a mile."

"I think," I said carefully, "I think you mean stock." Marlon Maykout— I remembered it from Nosey's information— was a stock broker. Sort of. But mainly just a thief. "So he came and then… what?"

"Mostly nothing," Pansy said. "At first he's just

standing there and fooling around the door which was anyway half-open, going 'Rex? Rex? You there? Listen, Rex, I haven't forgotten.'"

"Forgotten what? Did he ever say?"

"As I remember it," Pansy prattled, "after that, what he said was '*OH!*' Like he sees the blood and he does the *OH!* And during the *OH!*, Marietta comes in, and then it's the two of them doing the *OH!* And then after that, she was telling him, 'Wait! Don't make a phone call! Don't make a move!' And then she goes racing around like a fruitycake— into the bedroom, into the den— and then she comes out again, howling, 'Curses! Somebody stole it,' and then, after that—"

"She picked up the telephone," Catsby finished. "And, as you predicted, she called the police."

I thought for a moment, and glanced at the desk and the clutter of notebooks that sat on the top. "Was it Marietta who pulled out the notebooks?"

"No," Catsby said. "I'm afraid it was I. I thought they'd have something to do with the book. But, alas, there was nothing. Or nothing really. Just scribbles and dribbles with nobody's names, or no one we know of." He yawned in his paw. "Though, of course, he'd have changed them."

Pansy said, "Why? I mean why would he change them?"

"So's not to get sued." I glanced at the handwriting under her haunches and said, "Could you move it? I mean, just a bit?"

She obliged me with inches. I started to read:

Norma Jhelton was one of those women who
I first met Norma Jhelton on a sunny September morning

63

It was one of the two Wilsons who introduced me to Norma Thelton

Over a year before I met her, I'd heard the rumor that Norma Thelton

I first met Thadeus Wilson...

"That's a writer's block," I said. "Like he's trying to start a chapter but he can't even write a line. Is the rest of the stuff the same?"

"Even stupider," Pansy said. "And we've read about seven notebooks. There are only a couple left."

I said I'd help them and grabbed a book. A lot of ridiculous half-sentences: *Call me suspicious...Call me crazy.... Call me Ishmael...Call me a cab....*I flipped the book to the final entry:

Desperation! Utter Despair!
Are you serious, Rex? / I am.
Then show me you're serious, Rex. / I will.

SH	10	J/J	X X X X
X	2	F/A	X X X X
BB	15	M/S	X X X X
TP	5	A/O	X X X X
PS	20	M/N	X X X
SM	10	J/D	X X X

I showed it to Pansy. "It's some kind of code. Does it make any sense to you?"

"Not in the least."

"Could those be initials," I asked, "of people? I mean, of the people he put in the book?"

Pansy was squinting. She ran her paw on the first row of letters and squinted again. "Do you mean the S.H. or you mean the J. J.?"

"Do you know an S.H.?"

"But I know a J.J." She looked up at Catsby, who lowered his head. For a time he was silent, observing the blotter as though it had magnets that locked on his eyes. Then he lifted them slowly. "*Jay*-Jay," he said, "is a wonderful, wonderful, wonderful man. If he has any secrets, they're secrets of good and not secrets of evil or anything bad. If you think he's a killer—" He looked at me sharply.

I shook my head quickly. "I know that he's not. The shots were at two," I said, surer than ever. "At two we were watching him sleep at the pool. I looked at his wristwatch: ten after two."

Catsby said, "Perfect," and grinned his relief.

"But whatever this *is* —" I looked down at the notebook—"it's something important to do with the case. What I need is a copy."

"But why a copy? Just take the original. Tear out the page and then—"

"Carry it back in my mouth through the woods?"

"I can see the problem there," Catsby agreed.

"Like he'd get it all spittly and yucky and torn." Pansy looked at the paper. "I wish we could write. I mean, if we could, we could write him a copy. You think we could type it?"

I looked at the Royal. It wasn't so much that the keys needed pounding, but harder than that would be moving the lever that shuttled the carriage and moved the machine so whoever was typing could type a new line. And we didn't have paper. I looked at the code. There was no way to memorize all of those numbers and all of those letters and all of those checks. And without a computer, an e-mail was out.

I thought for a moment and happened to glance at the elderly fax machine next to the wall. Yes, that would do it.

I batted the phone and then punched out the numbers engraved in my heart. As I heard it ringing, I pictured the phone on the far other end of it, back in Manhattan, on top of the counter at Kitten Kaboodle where Sue would be sleeping— my redheaded Sue.

I waited it out while Harry, the owner, recited the usual pitch of machines: "This is Kitten Kaboodle, grooming and boarding. Please leave a message and have a nice day."

I started with "Sue? If you're there, pick up. It's extremely important."

I counted to ten. "Oh Sammy, *Sammy*," she purred, "is it you? Do you miss me awfully?"

I said, "I do."

"Did you call to tell me?"

I said, "I did. And I'll call you later to tell you how much. but right at the moment I'm needing a favor."

She snapped, "A favor."

I said, "It's small, but it's very important. I'm here on a case and I—"

"Leave it to *you*," she said tartly. "A case. A normal person would simply relax and just play in the sunshine and eat like a pig."

"Have I ever been normal?"

She said, "You've a point. So what is it this time? A stolen necklace? A missing kitten? A—"

"Murder," I said. I looked up at Pansy who looked so distressed that I added a "maybe" and rushed through the rest. "If I sent you a fax," I said quickly and softly, "you think you could scan it and send me an e?"

"I don't understand you," she said. "You want me to send you an e-mail of something you have?"

"Well, I have but I haven't," I said. "Can you do it? I promise I'll call you again in an hour."

"And you'll tell me you miss me?"

"I do and I will."

I clicked off the phone and then sat for a second, thinking I'd missed her much more than I'd known, and then Catsby said, "Brilliant! A brilliant idea." He was already ripping the page from the notebook. We trotted it over and faxed it to Sue.

12

By the time I got back to Hunnicker's it was nearly two in the morning and the only sounds in the house were the snorts and snorings behind his door. And of course his door was entirely closed. Which meant his computer, with all my e-mails, was out of combat, at least for the night. I paced the hallway in deep frustration. I wanted answers. I wanted clues. I wanted progress. I wanted...food.

I went to the kitchen, remembering something my mother had told me was Rule Number One in her *General Rules for a Happier Life*. "Whenever in doubt," she'd instructed, "eat." I found a plate with some crumbled meatloaf and bits of kibble arranged on the floor on a tidy placemat. I ate, and drank from a bowl of water. My doubt was gone.

It was perfectly easy. I'd simply remember the rhyme that I'd written and take it from there. I curled on the counter and started to think. The first thing I thought of was Zelda Stardust who'd quite unspecifically "Done Things." And the blasted "Things" had been rhymed with...? Mings! Someone or other had stolen Mings! A Tippy Fraggle. A Mona Tapp. A Roger Higby. A...*Harold Rigby*. A Harold Rigby had torched his office. Or shot his husband. Or broke his socks. I was getting stupid. I needed sleep.

The dream I dreamed took me back to Nosey's. I sat in his office and typed on his Mac. I saw myself typing and looked at the screen. I read my typing. I read it twice.

Harold Rigby	Burned Building
Tippi Tapp	Stole Mings
Mona Fragg	Shot Husband
Zelda Stardust	Did Things.
Catsby's Roommate	Total Phony
Marlon Maykout	Phony Stocks
This could either be	Baloney
Or with luck,	It might be Lox.

I woke smiling. I had the list. If those, in fact, were the actual suspects, I could easily cancel three. Zelda and J.J. had been at the pool. And if Marlon Maykout had been at the cottage and buried the body and burgled the book then why would he visit again in the evening? Why would he come again, hollering "Rex? I haven't forgotten" and bang on the door? To establish an alibi? Well, to whom? To Catsby and Pansy? It didn't wash. So my possible suspects were down to three if I wasn't including Mysterious Strangers with terrible timing and lousy toupés.

I raced to the living room, jumped to the table and batted the speakerphone off of its hook and then waited through Harry and waited for Sue.

"Did you get my e-mail?" she asked.

I told her I couldn't get *to* it, at least for the night. "But, hey, if it's handy," I said, "could I ask you a couple of questions?"

She sighed. "Go on."

"Take a look at the columns with all the initials and see if they match with the following names: Harold Rigby..."

"An H R?" A moment of silence. "*Uh*-uh," she said. "And I hope you'll explain this."

"I will when I'm done." I quickly recited the rest of my list, getting "Nopes" and "Uh-uhs" for every name.

"Would you like to explain now?"

I would and did. The entire story came tumbling out, from the very beginning and up to the end. "I was almost certain the code would have something or other to do with the folks in the book."

"And what if it did?" she said. "Where would it get you?"

"Well, it would show me the poem was correct."

"Because if it isn't, you're nowhere at all?"

I said, "Exactly."

She said, "But Sam! There's a whole other part to the idiot code." She paused and yawned. "If it's even a code. I mean there's the numbers and all of the checks. I think you should look at the numbers and checks."

"And that's why I asked you to send me the scan."

"And that's why I sent it. Because you asked."

I said, "I miss you."

She said, "Go on."

"With how much I miss you?"

She said, "Of course."

"I missed you this morning," I said, "and this

70

evening. I'd like to have taken you off to the party and danced in the moonlight and shared all the fish. And I miss you right now when I need you to tell me I'm not being stupid and chasing a goose."

"You're *not* being stupid," she said. "And a goose chase is probably better than no chase at all. And, besides that, the code could be unrelated."

"Or maybe the code could be some kind of code."

"Well of *course* the code could be some kind of code." She was losing patience. "A code's a code."

"Unless, of course, it's a *double* code."

"And what on earth is a double code?"

"It means the code is a code for a code."

"You've lost me completely," she said, and paused. "Are you stoned on catnip?"

"I haven't touched it since Harry's party on New Year's Eve and even at that, I was totally sober."

"You rolled on the floor and you sang like a loon and did Garfield impressions."

I said, "Were they good?"

She said, "Actually, yes."

I said, "Back to the code." I said, "Rex's novel itself is in code. It's the actual stories of actual people except that he's given them fictional names."

"You mean something like code names."

"Exactly," I said. "So if Harold Rigby is Steven Higby, his coded initials are—"

"S.H.. But you couldn't prove that without the book and the book has been stolen."

I said, "I know. So I'm hoping you're right that the clue's in the numbers. I'll look at the numbers as soon as I can."

"Well you've got until Monday," she said. "I assume

you'll be coming home again Monday night?"

"That's what Hunnicker promised." I looked at the clock. It was Sunday morning at 3:21. I had forty-two hours to wrap up the case or go home as a failure. I cringed at the thought.

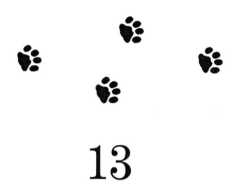

13

I spent the night at the edge of the porch under billions of stars and a man-faced moon and I slept a profound and refreshing sleep. The tap that woke me was soft but insistent. I opened my eyes in a dazzle of sun and, after a second of total confusion, I blinked at the tapper. I managed, "Tom?"

"I'm sorry to wake you," he said. "I figured you'd want to know that the cops were at Doc's."

I yawned and stretched and awakened my brain. "So how did they know about Rex's appointment?"

"They found a prescription in Rex's car. Remember how Flo said he'd got a prescription? It's dated yesterday, day of the crime. So the cops come knocking. They're asking questions. They ask the Doc, "Did you take any blood?" and the Doc goes to get it and says that it's gone. That he guesses his nurse took it off to the lab which is closed until Tuesday."

I said, "Uh-huh."

"So why were they asking? I mean for the blood."

I yawned again, and looked out at the hedges that marked the beginning of Catsby's estate. "To see if it matches the blood in the house. Did they track the nurse down?"

"She went to the city. The doctor told them he didn't know where."

"So that's the end of it now till Tuesday."

Tom shrugged indifferently. "Yeah. I guess. You can go back to sleep now. Unless..."

"Unless?"

"Well I thought I'd go fishing," he said, "in the bay. The cops were all over it, all through the morning, but now that they've finished, I figured I'd fish. If you'd want to come with me..."

"What time is it?"

"Noon?"

I looked at the sun and agreed it was noon. I ought to get cracking, I thought, on the case. But the air was delicious. It tasted of flowers and sunned-upon grasses, and sweet little birds, and the notion of catching my very own breakfast....I blurted impulsively, "Right. You're on," and we raced to the lawn in a boisterous hurry, eager to savage the summoning shore.

We were half into grass when I heard the footsteps, the sound of voices, the muted blips of an officer's radio: *"Car twenty-seven. A minor disturbance at Annabelle Lane...."* I stood at attention and swiveled my ears. The noises were coming from Catsby's hedges. Tom shot a look at me. "What's going on?"

"We'll know when we get there," I said, and we both made a change in direction and raced to the hedge and then wedged ourselves into it, peering through leaves.

From where we were hiding, I made out the shoes and the navy blue trousers of several cops and the water-splashed tiles that surrounded the pool. A cop-voice was barking, "Are you Mr. Smythington?"

J.J's response came from somewhere beyond. "What can I do for you?"

"Well, to begin with, we'd like you to get yourself out of that pool, and then answer some questions."

"Sure. About what?" Splishes and splashes. A deep-throated grunt. The slapping of barefooted steps on the tile. Then J.J. Smythington's slightly hairy, but evenly suntanned and well-muscled legs.

"This is Officer Peters, I'm Officer Krupp."

"Uh-huh. Okay. And you're here about what?"

"It's about where you were at five-thirty last night."

A second of silence. "I'd guess in my car."

"And what were you doing?"

"You mean in my *car*? I'd guess I was driving."

"Funny. Where?"

"Nowhere particular. Driving around."

"Uh-huh. Around. Around Featherstone Road?"

"That's possible, Officer. Possibly, yes."

"Your car was observed there at five-twenty five."

"Then I'd probably been there."

"And why did you go?"

"I didn't *go* there. I'm driving around."

"And you possibly drove there."

"I possibly did."

"And you possibly parked and went into the woods?"

"In fact, I parked and went into the woods. What are you driving at?"

"Why were *you*?"

"What?"

"Driving."

"I felt like a drive."

"All of a sudden, you felt like a drive."

"Is suddenly driving against the law?"

"But lying to cops is against the law."

A terrible silence. A terrible sigh. Then, "Somebody called me and told me to meet him."

"And where did you meet him?"

"He wasn't there."

"And where was the there where you didn't meet him?"

"Out in the woods off of Featherstone Road."

"And who was the somebody?"

"Well... I don't know."

"You don't know his identity."

"Sorry, I don't."

"A Mysterious Stranger."

"All right. If you like."

"And why did this stranger request that you meet?"

"The stranger had something of mine that was stolen. He said he'd return it."

"A 'something.' Right. And what's my next question?"

Another pause. "Do I want a lawyer?"

"That wasn't the question."

"It might be the answer."

"You think?"

"I dunno. It depends why you're asking."

A terrible pause and then J.J.'s toes seemed to twitch on the tiles. The second officer finally spoke. "Well, Mr. Smythington, here's how it goes. There's a bad-looking crime scene on Featherstone Road. There's blood on the carpet, there's shots in the wall and there's star-spangled footprints on part of the path and a clock that was stopped there at twenty to six."

"And a missing person," the first cop said. "We imagine you know him. A Rexford Trout?"

"Well of course I know him. In fact—"

"We know. He bugged on your party. But here's why we ask. At dawn this morning, we dragged the bay and we pulled up a boat that was purposely sunk. And we pulled up a gun and a nice pair of sneakers and guess what they're wrapped in? A bloody rug."

"You pulled up a gun."

"We pulled up the handgun that blasted the bullets that stuck in the clock and a nice pair of sneakers with stars on the soles. And oh, by the way. They had nice little name tags with someone's initials. You know whose they were? I believe the initials were J.J.S."

Another silence. Another sigh. I looked over at Tom who was pawing the ground, looking ready for battle. I shook my head No.

"That gun," J.J. said, "was the 'thing' that was stolen."

"Uh-huh....Mr. Smythington, here's how it goes. You have the right to remain silent. You have the right—"

"Am I under arrest?"

"No. Not exactly," the first cop said. "But you'd better get dressed and come down to the station."

"But listen. I didn't—"

"Uh-huh. Let's go."

The legs— all six of them— started to move. I waited a second and poked through the hedge: Off to my left, the retreating J.J. flanked by the twosome of

Serious Cops. And off to my right, a deflated Catsby, alone and alarmed, at the edge the pool. He appeared to be frozen, his eyes to the ground. Then he lifted his head up and angled his tail up and yowled like a loon at the pitiless sky.

14

I have to admit to a peeve about yowling. First, if not worst, it accomplishes nothing. It rankles the neighbors. It's bad PR. But, further than that, it's an absolute downer, a noisy confession of infinite woe that can lead you to feel like a motherless kitten—lost and helpless and weak and small—on the very occasion you need to be strong. Time and energy wasted on yowling is time and energy much better spent on devising the dirty and devilish doom of whatever it was that was making you yowl. (I make an exception for giant hair-balls; a ratcheting yowl puts them out on the rug.)

"If you're *done*—" I said patiently and pointedly to Catsby, "we can get down to business here and start to clear his name."

Catsby stopped yowling and replaced it with a "Pshaw!"

"*Pshaw?*" I said. "*Pshaw?* What's *that* supposed to mean?"

"That *we*—" he said, squinting back and forth from

me to Tom and then curling up his lip, "are just *cats*, is what it means."

"Just cats," I said flatly. "Meaning cats who are just?"

"Oh stop it," Catsby said. "You know exactly what I mean. And I mean it's unlikely we can do a darn thing."

"Oh ho. Is it *really* now?" Tom was incensed. "I suppose," he said dryly, "you can speak for your chicken self. And then, while you're expanding on it, go lay an egg."

Catsby looked wounded.

Tom didn't care. "Man," he said angrily, "it drives me up a wall. Whenever I hear a mouser going, 'Oh, I can't deal with that, I'm only a little cat,' I want to puke on his velvet cushion. Get ahold of yourself. You're a cat! King of the jungle! Lord of the night!"

"A little bit smaller," I said, "but smart."

"And a natural hunter." Tom looked around. "This is some kind of mansion," he said with a sneer. "When a cat's in a mansion, he starts to get soft."

"I didn't *always* live in a mansion, I lived in an alley and then in a shelter and then in a walkup. I'm not any dude. As for what I *am*," Catsby said, "I'm a realist. I know my limits."

"You don't know *mine*," Tom said rather snidely.

I rolled my eyes up and looked at the sky. I didn't know if they knew they were rivals—potentially rivals for Pansy's paw—but I hoped they didn't. I needed their minds to be free of distraction and glued to the case. I said, uninflectedly, "Where's Pansy?"

"She slept in my cathouse. She's perfectly safe but completely exhausted. I left her some food." Catsby said it paternally. Tom didn't blink.

"Then she's taken care of," I said. "So now we can

80

get down to business. About that gun—"

"It was just like he told it." Catsby was carefully pacing the tiles and avoiding the puddles. "He got the phone call at just about five. He grabbed for some money and jumped in his car."

"And the gun had been stolen?"

"It certainly had. In fact, it's been stolen for several months. He'd given a party on April Fools' Day— as crowded a party as Saturday night's, except that it started at just about noon. And the morning after, the pistol was missing. He knew someone took it but didn't know who. And it could have been anyone. Servant or guest."

"And he didn't report it? I mean, at the time?"

"It wasn't registered. Not in New York."

I thought for a moment and studied my tail. "So I'd have to conclude that the person who called him's the person who took it." I squinted at Tom. "And had already used it."

"You mean...like at Trout's?" Tom looked inquisitive. "Still, if that's true, then he wouldn't return it."

"He couldn't," I said. "By the time of the phone call, he didn't have it. He'd already scuttled the thing in the bay."

Tom looked at Catsby who, slightly distracted, had sprawled in the overhead shade of a chaise. "Does that make any sense to you?"

Catsby said, "No. I can see why he dumped it but not why he called."

They both looked expectantly into my eyes which I quickly averted to look at the pool. The water was pretty, an aquamarine with a dappling of sunlight that floated in rings. It was almost hypnotic. I mumbled, "Unless..."

They almost pounced at me. "Yes? Unless?"

"Unless…" I punted, "unless the phone call was simply to get him to Featherstone Road so his car could be seen there at twenty to six."

"You mean so's to frame him?"

I nodded. "Yep. But I'm merely supposing." I paused and thought. The Mysterious Stranger— the one that I knew of, the one that was formally known as McGee— had been seen leaving town on the four o'clock bus. But he still could have cell-phoned at just about five…. "But then, on the *other* paw—"

"Hold it. Wait. You're skipping the *first* paw." Tom was annoyed, though whether at me or the puddle of water he'd absently stepped in, I couldn't be sure. Still, I explained about Mr. McGee, the Mysterious Stranger who'd stayed at the Ham and been seen on his bicycle coming from Trout's —or conceivably Trout's— and at just about three.

"If the shots were at two," Catsby said, "there'd be time to get rid of the body and bike into town and then pick up his luggage and get on the bus."

"But then on the *other* paw—" Now they were both of them watching me eagerly. "Listen," I said, "there's Mysterious Strangers from here to the moon. I mean strangers are strangers. There's people you know and then everyone else is Mysterious Strangers."

"Because you don't know them?"

"Exactly," I said. "Which makes them mysterious. Say someone phones and you don't know his voice and you don't know his name. So how'd you describe him?"

"Mysterious stranger." Tom looked at Catsby. "I think what he means is it could have been anyone."

"That's what I mean. And since Mr. McGee is beyond our control, I suggest we forget him, at least for a while, and start looking at others, like people in town who were known to have motives."

"And that would be who?" Tom looked expectant and Catsby, the skeptic, was rather impatiently cocking his head. I silently summoned the words of my poem. *Harold Rigby: Burned Building. Tippi Tapp: Stole Mings...* But Tippi Tapp was a thieving lady and J.J's caller, he'd said, was a man...

"Like Harold Rigby," I said, "for one."

"You mean *Georgia's* Rigby?" Catsby was stunned.

I simply gawped at him. "Georgia's living with Harold Rigby?"

He said, "Of course."

"And you know where the house is?"

He said, "Come on."

15

Rigby's house wasn't far from Pansy's. We took the shortcut that led through the woods. I looked for Virgil. He wasn't there, but he'd carefully drizzled the side of his tree and his personal scent was as clear as a sign: *PRIVATE PROPERTY! NO TRESPASSING! BACK IN AN HOUR! STRANGERS BEWARE!*

Lieutenant Catsby— Catsby was suddenly doing a War Movie scene in his head— had self-importantly taken the lead. He was several yards ahead of us, and bossy about it, too. He'd insisted on our marching in an orderly single file and gave instructions to "watch your tails." It was actually pretty silly—this was Ham not Nam— and all the "stop, drop and listen" stuff was comically out of hand but then Catsby was being driven by the libelous charge of "hen" and felt the pressure to prove otherwise. I had to give him a pass.

He slowed after a while and then turned and looked back at me. "So why Harold Rigby?"

"He's an arsonist," I said.

"You mean he burned his own building?"

"Or so Nosey says. And if Rex had discovered it..."

"I gotcha," Catsby said.

"So the heart-pounding question is: Was Rigby at the party? And I'm talking about the party where the pistol disappeared."

"Oh indeed." Catsby stopped and allowed me to catch up with him before traveling on. "I remember him quite clearly. In fact—" he was grinning rather cheer-fully— "I bit him."

"You didn't!" I said. "Why?"

"He was messing with J.J.'s watch. I think you saw it. Down at the pool?"

"Eighteen karat," I said. "A Rolex. And worth a fortune.— Messed with it how?"

"The way it happened was, J.J's swimming. He'd left his Rolex out on the chair. So Harold Rigby was picking it up. Like he's pretending to look at the time but he's looking around in case somebody's watching."

"You thought he'd steal it?"

"I thought he might."

I stopped in silence.

Catsby said, "What?"

"So if J.J. was *swimming*," I said, "then he wasn't wearing his sneakers."

"Well certainly not."

"So where were his sneakers?"

Catsby looked up. He stopped advancing and dropped his jaw. "Well, now that I think of it— under the chair!"

"So Harold Rigby—" I didn't finish.

From somewhere behind us, Tom did a "*Yowwww!*"

We turned and stared at him. Standing frozen, a

furry bump on a fallen log, his body strained in the shape of a horseshoe, he boggled, googly-eyed, at a snake. The greenish monster, who looked improbably like a garden hose with a head, was wriggling up to him, tongue darting, and making a sound like expiring tires.

"Don't try to frighten him!" Catsby commanded. "Don't even look at him! Don't move!"

"How about screaming?" Tom looked at Catsby.

"I wouldn't try it," was Catsby's response. "It's a Voodoo-Koodoo. A deadly killer. I read all about it in Saturday's *Times*."

I looked at him sideways but Catsby's focus was fixed with intensity off to the right. He crept there slowly. I stayed where I was. Tom didn't move. The snake didn't stop. It hissed and wriggled. Tom didn't breathe. I glanced at Catsby. A fallen branch, about seven feet long, was arranged on the ground. It was thin and pointy. Catsby approached it. Then he crouched over it. Then he lay still. Then he was squinting—the look of a pool player lining a shot up and suddenly... *Pow!* he was firing his weapon, pushing it, shoving it, poking it, prodding it into the snake who turned in amazement and slithered away.

"*Run for your life, Tom!*" Catsby suggested, and Tom made a practically vertical leap and then raced like a jackrabbit out of the woods and a half-mile ahead of us, out to the road.

Catsby looked up at me. "Not poison. Perfectly harmless."

I said, "You're a rat."

He grinned at me slyly. "But who's the chicken?"

****

86

Tom was subdued but surprisingly poised. He led the platoon across Featherstone Road and, skipping the driveway to Rex's cottage, he ran to the back of it, down to the shore and then followed the shoreline that curved to the left. We passed by the houses of Rex's neighbors and neighbors' neighbors and right after that, he said, "Harold Rigby's," and pointed up. I followed his gesture and looked up the slope of a grass-covered knoll to the back of a house. Then I focussed again on the tree-rimmed shoreline. Yes, if he'd wanted to, Harold Rigby could surely have snuck his way over to Trout's— could've taken a short-cut through silent gardens, or clung to the waterline, hidden by trees. In J.J.'s sneakers.

Catsby said, "Swell. We're at Harold Rigby's. So what's the plan?"

I didn't have one. I stalled for a moment and scratched at my whiskers and scratched at my chin and then scratched at my shoulders and said, "The plan.... The *plan*," I said slowly, "is planning the plan."

"Are you planning to plan it?"

"I'm planning it now." I looked at the tree line and up at the house. "Tom, when you told me you'd seen Rex's novel, you told me you'd seen it in some kind of box. Get into the house now and look for the box. And Catsby—" I squinted. "Go look for a grave. I mean look for a grave that's been recently dug. I mean, look in the flower beds. Look in the trees."

"But we figured the body'd been dumped in the bay."

"But the cops didn't find it." I stared at the shore. "All they found were the sneakers, the rug, and the gun."

"So you figure it's buried?"

I said, "I don't know. But it's worth looking into."

He sighed. "I suppose," and then somewhat reluctantly turned to his task.

Which left me and Tom to start casing the house. It was, to my thinking, surprising modest, though "modest" in Ham was a few million bucks. If you added the waterfront view, it was five. It was two stories high and entirely made out of brown wooden shingles with white wooden trim. A black iron rooster was perched on a pole at the pointiest pitch of the brown-shingled roof, turning slowly in circles— a toy of the wind. At the side was a sun room— a glass-enclosed porch with a door and a cat door— and in it, relaxed on a fern-patterned sofa, was Georgia, asleep.

Tom pointed left at a half open window that led to a kitchen. I nodded. "Go on.— Take it," I offered.

"And what about you?"

"My job is to waken the sleeping beauty."

Tom cackled loudly and said, "With a kiss?"

I shot him a look that could freeze Guatemala.

He leapt to the window.

I plunked to the porch.

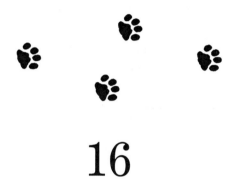

16

The couch, on which Georgia lay curled in a little ball, was the only non-vegetable item in the room which was otherwise devoted to a few million plants. It seemed Mr. Rigby had a thing about plants. The glass-panelled porch was an indoor Eden—a landscape of flowerpots bursting with flowers that exhaled their contentment in a sweet-smelling wave as they lazily lapped up their lunch from the sun. I wondered at once if a plant had a taste bud, and whether it savored the taste of the sun and what did sun taste like and would it taste better with Tobasco or jam. *Are you finished?* I asked myself. *Get back to work.*

I looked up at Georgia— a real piece of work. But beyond that impression, there was not much to think. I could think she was gorgeous (and she was, and I did) and I admired her sleeping body with its subtly rounded curves and the charming way she slumbered with her tail between her teeth. But when you finally got down to it, Georgia, fast asleep in the cocoon of her beautiful blondness was a lot more entertaining than Georgia awake. And I did have to wake her.

I noisily cleared my throat. Nothing. Not a twitch. I sneezed. She didn't move. I looked slowly around the room. A large empty Coke can was lying across the floor. I decided to wake it up. With a perfectly-placed place-kick, I whammed it across the room and watched it rattle its way bumpily and *whack* on the opposite wall.

Georgia woke suddenly and blinked in the bright sun. "Why, it's Sam the detective! What a scrumptious surprise!" She languidly lifted a long luscious leg and then lavishly licked it. "I do wish you telephoned first," she said coyly. "I fear when I'm wakened, I'm an absolute mess."

"Oh Georgia," I laughed, "You have never been a mess for one second of your life. And I'm sorry I had to wake you but I needed to see you."

"Needed?" she purred. "But that sounds so romantic."

"It isn't," I mumbled. "This is business right now."

"Tell me what kind of business. Funny business?"

"No. Just ordinary everyday crime-busting business. I was wondering—"

"Then wonder a little closer," Georgia said. She was tapping at the sun-spattered cushion at her side. "You can jump," she said huskily, and cocked her pretty head. "You *do* know how to jump, Sam, don't you?" I jumped.

She was gorgeous, all right. Close up, I could have drowned in the perfume of her glowing fur— that extraordinary aroma of a rich and exotic woman mixed with Fancy Feast Tender Bits of Turkey in Special Sauce.

"Still wondering?" Georgia crooned.

"About yesterday. In the morning." I attempted to hold my breath. "When you left us at Pansy's cottage, you announced you were going home. So the question would be: Did you?"

"Absolutely. I never lie. I am painfully, and often quite nastily, honest."

"I can picture that," I said.

"It doesn't always go over big."

"Well, relax," I said soothingly, "it's doing the trick now. So what time did you get home?"

"What's *time*," she said, "to a cat? I mean, why would I even notice? Like it's dinnertime or it's not."

"Well, let's try it another way. How long would you say it takes you to get from Pansy's place to here?"

"Maybe just a couple of minutes, Sam." She licked at her lovely paw. "But I know when I left there it was twelve twenty-seven."

"And how do you know *that*?"

"Because it said so on Pansy's clock."

Pow-*BAM*! It suddenly hit me. Well, of course! The grandfather clock! The clock had been ticking— loudly and grimly— while Pansy'd explained about the flounder and the duck. So the clock had been working then at twelve twenty-seven. I filed it away under *Bullets in Clock*.

I said: "When you got here, was Rigby at home?"

"He was taking a shower."

"You're certain?"

"He sings."

"And after he finished," I said, "did he leave?"

"I wouldn't think so," she said. "I didn't exactly see him with actual eyes. But then I figured he's in the den. I mean the Yankees were playing baseball and he wouldn't've missed the game. It's like a thing he does with his friends. They all come over, they drink liquor, and eat pastrami and curse the screen."

"And did you happen to see or hear them?"

"I try not to." She shook her head. "I went to the garden. But why do you ask?"

"It's just a habit," I said. "Whenever I start to wonder, I start to ask."

"And what do you wonder," she said, "about me?" Her little nose made a pass at my ear and then nuzzled my shoulder and blew on my neck. I could feel myself melting. I summoned my will.

"Georgia, Georgia, " I said, and sighed. "You leave so little to wonder *about*."

"And why *should* I?" she said.

"Because…." I tried to gather my words precisely, "because romance is all in the mind. It's a mental preoccupation. Like a puzzle. Like a dream. Like a brightly-ribboned Christmas present sitting up in the closet and inviting you to wonder."

"Then wonder something, please."

I rose rather heavily and looked her straight in the eye. "I wonder—" I whispered to her, "why were you asking me if Rigby was in the book. Remember? During Catsby's party last night."

"Did I really? Well I don't remember asking that at all. But then he *might've* been in the book. I mean anybody might."

"But why Harold Rigby?"

She shrugged with both paws.

"How about because he set his building on fire?"

"Oh that," she said. "But that was forever ago, I

think. And besides, he didn't do it."

"He didn't?"

"Not himself. I heard him planning it on the phone. He had somebody else do it."

I stared at her. "And who was that 'somebody'? Do you know?"

"Just a somebody on the phone."

"Or in other words," I sighed, "a mysterious stranger."

She nodded. "I suppose."

"Perhaps the same stranger that he ordered to kill Trout?"

"Oh my goodness!" Georgia gasped. "He wouldn't ever commit a murder. I mean he wouldn't commit a *crime*."

"You mean arson isn't a crime?"

"Not exactly," she said. "It's different. I mean the building belonged to Rigby and he did what he had to do."

"You mean to cover his other crime."

"People do what they have to do. What they have to do to survive. In fact I think it was rather clever. Like the time I accidentally knocked the candy dish to the floor. Well, I didn't know what to do. I mean, I couldn't bury the pieces so I picked up the Yorkie's bone—we had a Yorkie here at the time— and then I carried it up where the dish had been and left it and went to sleep."

"And what happened?"

"Well...you don't see any Yorkies here, do you?"

I began to see what she meant. "No conscience?"

"Not in the least. I mean it's practical," Georgia said. "It's survival of the fittest. We have to face it,

Sam, we're living in a Cat Eat Dog world."

I thought it over. I thought we were but I've never thought we should act like beasts. If we act like beasts, we create a jungle, and all those billions of bloody years of slowly creeping towards civilization are lost and wasted. We're back in time, Neanderthal kittens without a clue about love and honor or trust and peace.

"I'd better get going." I noticed Tom had arrived in the garden, looking alert, and Catsby was chasing a mole on the grass.

"Will I see you later, then?" Georgia asked.

I jumped from the sofa and plopped to the floor. I turned and looked up at her. "Georgia," I said, "I think it's time to be perfectly honest. I've got a girlfriend back in the city—"

"Don't tell me you're *faithful*?" She looked amused.

I said, "I'm faithful."

She said, "You're a fool. And you couldn't *begin* to know what you're missing."

I said, "I do. And I'll see you later. I'll see you later to say goodbye."

"You can say it now," she said, suddenly bitter.

And so I said it. I said, "Goodbye."

17

We trotted silently down to the waterline and sat in the shade of a tree on a soft and comforting bed of grass. Tom was eager to give his report, which mainly consisted of "No boxes."

Catsby announced there were "No graves," but then added gravely, "I found a bone."

I cocked my ears and said, "What kind of bone?"

"Come on. I'll show you."

He led us off to a circle of dirt by another tree, where the soil had been scratched into powdery mounds. In the narrow depression that Catsby had dug, was a notably small and inelegant bone, about four inches long, about two inches wide, with a number of teeth marks and fragments of dirt.

"It belonged to the Yorkie." Tom breathed a sigh. "Alas, poor Yorkie, I knew him well. He liked to rub noses and play on the grass. He must have buried it."

"Where did he go?"

"Mr. Rigby evicted him. Somebody said he went off

to the shelter but found a new home. He was one of the lucky ones."

Catsby looked down, perhaps in remembrance of shelters past and his own bit of fortune in finding J.J. We joined him in silence, a mournful moment for all of those others who'd run out of luck and who'd gone to their maker for innocent crimes like a baritone bark or a broken dish.

Catsby looked up at me. "You, I presume, have been talking to Georgia. So what did you learn?"

"That Harold Rigby, who didn't do it, was watching a ball game when Trout was shot." I added dryly, "Or that's her story."

"You think it's a story?"

I said, "Flip a coin."

Catsby glared at me. "Meaning *what*?"

"That fifty-fifty," I said, "it's a tale."

Tom laughed. Catsby didn't and appeared to be annoyed. "This is no time to pun," he said. "We're talking about a crime."

"And a *crime*," Tom injected rather glibly, "makes him pun-ish. But you're serious, Sam, aren't you. So why would she tell a lie? I mean, why would she lie for Rigby?"

"She wouldn't," I said, "for Rigby, but she'd lie to protect herself. If he's the killer, he'd go to jail, and I'm figuring Georgia—"

"Would go to the shelter." Catsby was nodding. "A reason to lie."

"But then, on the *other* side of the coin," I said, "suppose she's telling the truth. I mean suppose it's at least possible that Rigby's watching the game and has a witness or two to prove it. What I'm telling you is, he—"

96

"*Hold it!!*" Tom was excited. "I think he was."

I looked at him skeptically. "Why do you say?"

"Come up to the window," he said. "Have a look."

We raced to the house and then leapt to a sill and then peered through the glass at a comfortable den where a long leather sofa was facing a wall. Up on the wall was a seven-foot screen. Down on the sofa, the cushions were dented. I started counting them. Seven dents. So seven bottoms had dented the couch. But the meatier clue (and the pun is intended) was found in the plates that were scattered around and held shreds of pastrami and crumpled napkins and ends of pickles and crusts of bread. There were also beer bottles—three times seven— and bits of potato chips ground on the rug.

"Who says it was Saturday's?" Catsby muttered.

"I ate some pastrami." Tom flicked his tail. "It wasn't today's, but it wasn't ancient. I'd say it was Saturday's."

"Possibly so." I leapt from the window and back to the ground. "But he still could have stolen the shoes and the gun and then paid off a stranger to finish the job."

"The Mysterious Stranger?"

"I couldn't be sure, but it looks a lot likelier."

Tom shook his head. "This is getting us nowhere. The Stranger is gone and we couldn't connect him to Harold Rigby."

I nodded grimly. "Or anyone else." I walked in a circle and pawed at the ground. I'd entirely blown it. I'd bungled the case. I hadn't even thought about the obvious possibility that one of my six suspects would have hired somebody else. As they certainly would have.

97

Beyond any doubt. These were people, after all, who could "do what they had to;" who could buy off the sheriff; who could silence the press; who could phone for a murder like you'd phone for a pizza while they rigged up an alibi to hide their own hand. So it wouldn't even help me to check them all out. Whoever was behind it (and I still had the feeling it was somebody on the list) would have three thousand witnesses who'd swear to their whereabouts from Christmastime to now.

"So—" Catsby looked at me, "so where do we go from here?"

"Go home," I said. "Both of you. Catsby, go to Pansy now, and Tom, go—" I almost blurted out, "go to Flo" but instead I said, "wherever."

"And you?" he asked.

I shrugged at him. "I haven't got a clue."

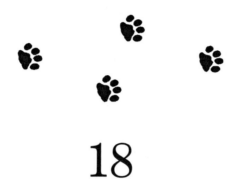

18

I sat for a while and just stared at the waterfront, trying to clear my head in a breeze that blew from the bay. The breeze smelled of sunshine. The sun smelled of sea. The shore birds were circling— soaring and swooping in an orbit around the sky but then returning to where they started. Was *I*, I began to wonder, merely circling like the birds? Was I moving but getting nowhere? Was I chasing my own tail? It didn't matter a lot, did it? As Georgia had just reminded me, we do what we have to do. Fish gotta swim and birds gotta fly. Crooks have to be crooked and detectives have to detect. And I had to go somewhere, even around in circles. So I rather reluctantly picked up my tail and went plodding into the circle. Very slowly, nose to the ground.

I followed the trees till they led me around to Pansy's, and, entering Pansy's, went quickly back to the den. The shots had been fired from its open doorway. I stood in the doorway and stared at the clock.

The clock had been ticking at 12:27. The shots had been aimed from the doorway at two. But the clock had been shattered at twenty to six. Or *appeared* to be shattered at twenty to six— over three hours later. So how could that be? The bullet, of course, could have jiggered the hands. But then, on the other hand, so could the shooter.

I tried to imagine the chain of events. Rex had come back here at just about one. Pansy and I had gone straight out the door so the house had been empty. So what happened then? I pictured the action.

Scenario One: Rex had gone out again. Stranger comes in. In J.J.'s sneakers. With J.J.'s gun. Stranger is busily burgling the den in his search for the novel when Rex enters house. Rex either sees or does not see the Stranger but Stranger sees Rex and then... bangety-bang. Stranger then frantically rifles the house. Stranger finds novel. Stranger disposes of Rex's body along with the sneakers, the gun and the boat and then swims to the house again and goes to the den where he steals Rex's pistol— the pistol that he happens to find in the drawer on the envelope printed with globe-sprouting-wings and he also takes envelope. Why? I don't know.

This is faintly preposterous. Maybe it's true but it's faintly preposterous. Try something else.

I tried something else's—three of them, in fact— but they all sounded stupid. I tried something else.

I leapt to the desk chair and stared at the desk. The lamp, which was lighted last night, wasn't on and the notebooks we'd plowed through were back in their drawer which was three inches open. I kicked at the drawer-pull and slammed the thing shut. The drawer underneath it popped open. Ker-*bang*. I leaned over slowly and kicked it back in, but as soon as I slammed it, the top drawer opened. I kicked it back in. The bottom drawer opened. I kicked it back in. I repeated this foolery three dozen times till it ceased to amuse me and bored me as well. This now left me staring with glazed-over eyes at the wide open pit of the bottom drawer.

It was just as I'd left it: The high school yearbook had slid past the phonebook and landed in front and I read, once again, on its blue plastic cover, the curious title of *Ozark High* and a year that would date it as seven years old. The book was too heavy to lift from its bed, so I dove down to meet it and sat in the drawer. I pawed the book open and read the first page:

> *Ozark High, named for Richard Ozark is, as we hail it, 100 years old and the fourth oldest high school in Kalamazoo...*

I paused for a moment. Kal-uh-muh-zoo. I liked how it sounded. Kal-uh-muh-zoo. I'd heard of it some-where but didn't know where and then—yes! I knew where. Zelda Stardust! Nosey had told me that Zelda Stardust had worked in a Starbucks in Kalamazoo. And that Rex had first met her (in Kalamazoo) and then brought her to Bigtown to launch her career. And Tom had informed me that Rex changed her name. From Starbucks to Stardust. Yes, it made sense.

I flipped through the year book and then, there she was. *Zelda Witorski.* I practically gasped. Zelda Witorski was as round as a beachball with so many zits you could barely see her face, except for the sad look of mourning in her eyes. Was this Zelda's "secret"? It wasn't any crime. In fact, it was awesome. A tribute to fantasy and sheer force of will. It was, in its outcome, the American Dream. Zelda Witorski had created Zelda Stardust out of high-fashion photographs and adolescent dreams and then worked to become her. I liked her for that. I closed up the yearbook. A photo fell out. Zelda, half-smiling at a Starbucks counter. Zelda, already the Zelda of today, except younger and shyer— the one Rex had met. But then why was he holding onto yesterday's Zelda? To use in his "novel"? I wasn't quite sure.

I quickly inspected the two other drawers— the first with the pencils and ribbons and dust, and the one underneath with the folded checkbook and the stack full of statements from the Hamilton Bank. I glanced through the checkbook, noting that Rex was a terrible accountant. The sums weren't totaled. The stubs were half blank and the rest were ho-hum: *Cable. Electric. Bloomingdale's. Cash.* What seemed to stand out were the monthly deposits: January: + $10,000. February: + $2000. Followed by a + $15,000 and, in April, another 5. Which added up to what? That Rex had a generous monthly income. Was that, for a resident of Ham, a surprise?

I sat there and thought till my head felt empty and my spirit felt low. Then I rose very purposely and raced to the woods.

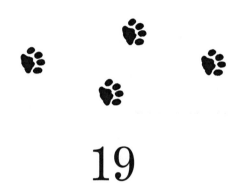

19

"Virgil?" I hollered.

"Yo," he said. "What?" He was standing there sniffing at the base of his tree, making sure no one'd bothered it. "Smelled you was here. You and them cats and that slime-bellied snake. Went from here on to Rigby's. You still on your case?"

"I am till tomorrow," I said, "when I leave."

"So you think Rigby done it?"

I shrugged. "I don't know. But he's likely got witnesses to swear that he didn't. And then there's the stranger. The guy on the bike? And the cops think it's J.J.—"

"The guy on the bike?"

"No, the guy on the *bike* is a guy named McGee. But the problem is—"

"Hold it, son, and wind it back down. You're talkin too fast and my ears ain't accustomed so I'm listenin slow. Take a breath," Virgil ordered, "and arrange your ideas."

I sat, very grateful for Virgil's advice and his fatherly patience. I laid out the facts. From start to finish. From Nosey and the poemful of suspects to now.

"I see," he said thoughtfully, and nibbled at his nail. "What you got here's some pieces but that ain't addin' up. And it seems like, to me, you got too *many* pieces. Like you can't see the forest for the twiglets on the trees."

"Very possibly," I sighed.

"So start the thing over now and tell me what you think."

"What I *think*?" I said wryly. "I can tell you what I *thought*. Except most, if not all of it, is strictly unthunk."

"Name seven," Virgil said.

"Well, I thought, to begin with, it was someone on the list and that all I'd have to do was check the people on list—and quite specifically the men—"

"Why specifically the men?"

"Because a man phoned J.J. And the sneaker-prints were large. And a man would have the strength to dump a body into the bay—"

"Except it *wasn't* in the bay."

"It wasn't *found* in the bay. Doesn't mean that it wasn't there. It could've floated out to the ocean."

"Coulda been et by a giant shark."

"Could've been buried in somebody's yard."

"Or he could've been luckier," Virgil said, "he could've survived it and swum to shore."

"I hadn't thought of that."

"Well, he might."

I thought it over and shook my head. "If he'd

104

landed safe, he'd've called the police. He'd've called the police and the national press. And boy, what an angle for selling his book."

Virgil just looked at me. "Well, I suppose. But I interrupted you. Where were you going?"

"I started to say I was probably wrong. That none of them did it. Or did it themselves. They hired a killer. The guy on the bike. He committed the murder at just about two, and then scuttled the body, and biked to the Ham and then got on the bus to Manhattan at four."

"And telephoned J.J.?"

I said, "Uh-huh." Then I thought for a moment and said, "Ah-*hah*!"

Virgil examined me. "What's 'ah-*hah*!'?"

"There's a double motive at play, Virgil. Whoever's behind it was not only frightened of Rex's novel and Rex himself but they hated J.J.. And very ingeniously plotted to frame him."

"And that'd be who?"

"I haven't the foggiest, Virgil. Sheesh."

"But you've narrowed it down to the murdering Stranger?"

I said, "I think so. I'm practically sure. But it doesn't help me. And worst of all, it's entirely useless in clearing J.J. I've totally muffed it," I said. "I've failed."

"Well, you didn't really. You got a notion. You got a notion that's pretty sweet so you probably solved it. At least in yer head."

"But the stuff in my head doesn't matter a bit. The stuff that matters is actual justice. And by the way, I could even be wrong."

"Well, you want my opinion—"

I said, "I do. I came here to see you to get your

opinion. I trust you, Virgil. I totally do."

"Well, I take that kindly," he said. "If ever I'd had a son, I'd've wished it was you. Intelligent fella. Solid as brass. But you want my opinion, I'd tell you, go home. Go lie in the sunshine and catch a few fish and go back to yer lady and rub at her nose and live happily, happily ever after. Life is a puzzle but life is short and you don't want to waste it on worries and woes. And especially those you can't hardly affect."

"Is that your secret?" I said.

"Of what?"

"Of being happy and living long."

"Well, I'd likely say so," he said. "I've lived to a hundred-and-twenty in humanly years, and I've liked every minute."

"Then keep it up."

"I have every intention of keeping it up. And my other secret is taking a nap. So you'll have to forgive me..." He stifled a yawn.

"Then I'll see you later," I said. "Goodnight."

20

"Have you solved the mystery?" Pansy asked. She'd come out to the doorway of Catsby's playroom and greeted me warmly by rubbing my nose.

"Well, not exactly," I had to admit. "In fact, to be straight with you, no, not at all. But I'm not giving up on it.— Catsby around?"

She angled her head towards the side of the house. "He's comforting J.J.. The cops let him go."

"I figured they'd have to," I said. "For a while. Till they turn up the... evidence."

Pansy sighed. "What you mean is the body," she added bravely.

"I meant the body," I answered. "Yes."

"Would you like to come in?" she invited.

"Sure." I entered the wonderfully magical room with the feathery bed and the painted birds. I sat on the floor while she curled on the bed.

"He's asked me to marry him." Pansy announced.

I suddenly grinned at her. "Hey, that's swell."

"So whatever happens, I'll have a home."

"And I guess you love him."

She fairly beamed. "I've always loved him," she said, "from the start. And I've missed him terribly. Every day. When we moved from Manhattan, I cried for a week, and I couldn't *imagine* he'd wind up in Ham. Of course—" she was giggling— "neither could he." She paused for a moment. "He says it was fate. I believe it was angels and lucky stars. Do you think there are angels and lucky stars?"

"On a few occasions," I said, "I do. When you can't explain it by rational logic, it has to be—"

"Angels and lucky stars." She nodded complacently.

"How did you meet?"

"It was perfectly lovely," she said.

"But how?"

"He lived in the tippermost top of a walkup. I lived in a condo, directly across, and my corner window looked right into his. We'd sit in our windows and talk and talk."

"You said in a walkup."

She nodded yes.

"Do you mean in a townhouse?"

"Oh heavens no. It was totally crummy. But Catsby loved it. He said there were plenty of roaches to chase and he said they were much more amusing than toys."

"Was he living with J.J. or somebody else?"

"Oh it was J.J. I used to see him. He'd come to the window and water the plants."

I scratched at my whiskers. "And what did he do? I mean, for a living?"

"I wouldn't know. And now that I think of it—" Pansy frowned — "I'm not even certain I knew his name. Catsby, I'm sure of it, called him 'my man.'"

"That's very interesting, Pansy."

"Oh?" She was suddenly yawning.

"I'll leave you alone."

"Shall I give him a message?"

"Yeah. You can tell him I wanted to see him. As soon as he can."

"And where can he find you?"

I gave it some thought. "In Hunnicker's bedroom," I said, "if I'm lucky."

"I'll tell him," she offered.

Forget about luck.

Forget about angels and lucky stars. I came out of the hedges and glanced at the house. And there was Hunnicker, practically pretzeling out of his window and sneaking a smoke. Hunnicker's sister— a girl who was much more devoted to fashion than brotherly love— had entirely banned him from smoking inside. So Hunnicker, technically, wasn't "inside," which I guess made them happy, at least in a way. Hunnicker's sister maintained the illusion of perfect compliance and Alpine air, and Hunnicker reveled in thumbing his nose.

This was ducky for them but disaster for me. My personal goal was to get to his bedroom and check out the laptop and dope out the code, which I couldn't accomplish with Hunnicker there, so I'd have to outwait him. I flopped on the porch. The sound of commercials came out of the den where The Sister sat crunching on salsa and chips, and occasionally belching. I moved to the steps to avoid the distraction and started to think.

I was thinking of J.J., who not very long ago lived in a walkup surrounded by bugs and who now owned a mansion. So what had he done? Was it angels and stars that had blessed him with fortune, or some kind of truly unspeakable crime, or the natural fruits of intelligent labor? And who had it in for him?

Catsby said, "Boo!" He stood on the pathway and angled his head. "You wanted to see me," he said.

"I did. I wanted to ask you a couple of questions. Like who hated J.J.."

He said, "Not a soul," and then sat down beside me and licked at his paws. "He's a wonderful person," he said, looking up.

"That has nothing to do with it. People are hated for all sorts of reasons. Like being too smart. Or being too handsome. Or being too rich. Does that ring any bells for you?"

"Not even one."

"Let me narrow the question. There's Harold Rigby. Did Harold hate him?"

Catsby said, "No. He hardly knew him."

"Or Marlon Maykout or Tippi Whatsis or Mona Fragg?"

"He barely talked to them."

"Still...they all of them came to his parties."

"But everyone did."

"Were the rest of those names at the gun-stealing party?"

Catsby said, "Probably. What's this about?"

I told him my theory: the double motive—the anger at J.J. as well as at Trout. He nodded slowly. "I guess you've a point."

"So how was J.J.? I mean, right now."

"He's pretty exhausted. He called a lawyer. He's ordering pizza. And that's about it. So what's in store for him?"

"Nothing good. They won't arrest him. At least not yet. And they couldn't officially call him a killer. They'll probably call him 'a person of interest.'"

"Which means?"

"A killer."

Catsby looked ill. "And what do they do to him?"

"Tail him around. They'll be crawling all over him. So will the press. And once it goes public, the public arrives. They'll be camped on your driveway. They'll sleep on your lawn. It's about to get noisy," I added, "and bad."

Catsby was silent and lowered his head.

"So what's his secret?" I suddenly blurted. "You might as well tell me. The press is a dog and they'll keep on digging. They'll find his bone."

Catsby looked up at me, sadly resigned. "You'll still have to swear that you'll never repeat it."

I lifted my paw and said, "Solemnly swear."

"Well…to begin with, he isn't J.J. And next, to begin with, it isn't his house. He's merely the care-taker."

"Oh of course. He's merely a lug with a fabulous watch and a famous girlfriend. An average Joe."

"It's a tricky story," he said.

"Go on. If he isn't J.J.," I said, "who is?"

"Will you let me *tell* it?" He sounded testy. "And stop interrupting?"

I said, "Go on."

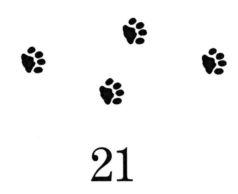

21

" **J**.J. Smythington—" Catsby rose and then started pacing the length of the porch— "is a wealthy fellow who comes from England. He comes from a township in middle Midlands, a little village called Sturgeon-on-Rye, although on *that* one, I think he was joking."

I simply squinted and said, "Ya think?"

Catsby ignored me and paced to the wall. "The actual point is, he comes from an ancient, historical family. Barons and earls. Castles and carriages. Mansions and moats. And the modern-day Smythingtons run a foundation. The Noble Foundation."

I stifled a laugh. "The *Noble* Foundation?"

"What's odd about that? They support Noble Causes."

"You mean give them money."

"I mean give them millions. And *don't interrupt.*"

I swore that I wouldn't. "But cut to the chase."

"Well it wasn't a *chase*," Catsby said, "but a fox hunt. His Uncle Sebastian was fatally shot when his sister mistook him for being the fox. But the upshot of *that* was, he died with a fortune— he left it to J.J., who lived in New York— but on one condition. That J.J. use it to start a foundation, called Noble West, and then live at this mansion and run its affairs."

I didn't comment. Catsby had paused at the top of the stairway and looked in my eyes. "I figured by now you'd be bursting with questions."

"My only question," I said, "is '*But... ?*'"

"*But...* the *point* is, he didn't want to. What he really wanted to *do* was to play guitar in a hot band."

"Instead of being a billionaire?"

"Did I say 'instead of'?"

"I take your point."

"Will you just be patient and hear me out? So it happens J.J.—*my* J.J.—who's actually Ted Parker— plays guitar in a hot band. And J.J.—the *real* J.J.— hangs around at The Papered Wall and—"

"That's a music club in the Village?"

Catsby nodded. "Where Ted played. So anyway, the up, down and short of it is, they switch. J.J.—the *real* J.J.— is on the road with the hot band, and *my* J.J.—"

"Ted Parker."

"—is living high in a gorgeous house and throwing parties for Noble Things."

"You mean his parties—"

"Collect for charities. Hungry children and home-less cats and a mess of diseases I couldn't pronounce."

"And this is forever? I mean, the switch?"

"Nothing's forever." Catsby looked down. "But J.J's happy. The little band made a couple of albums and had a few hits and they're playing in Vegas the last I heard."

"And how about Ted? Is Ted happy too?"

"Ted's getting serious, Sam. He always wanted to feel he was doing good and he seems to be good at the job he's doing. And having money, of course, is fun."

"And what would have happened if Rex exposed him?"

"I can't imagine. Except that J.J.—the *real* J.J.—would lose the money and who knows what. And then maybe both of them'd go to jail, though it isn't criminal. Nobody's hurt and then all of those causes are still being helped."

"That's quite a story," I said.

"It's true."

"It's too fantastic *not* to be true. I imagine it's—Hold it!" I held up a paw and then listened intently to noises inside. Yes, that was Hunnicker's voice in the den. He was out of his bedroom. I said, "Let's go."

"It's now or never," I said, as the two of us sat on the dresser and stared at the Mac. "We're either breaking the code or we're not."

I pulled up my poetry onto the screen and then pulled up the copy of Rex's code. We looked at the two of them side by side.

Harold Rigby	Burned Building	*SH*	*10*	*J/J*	*XXXXX*
Tippi Tapp	Stole Mings	*X*	*2*	*F/A*	*XXXXX*
Mona Fragg	Shot Husband	*BB*	*15*	*M/S*	*XXXXX*
Zelda Stardust	Did Things	*TP*	*5*	*A/O*	*XXXXX*
Catsby's roommate	Total Phony	*PS*	*20*	*M/N*	*XXXX*
Marlon Maykout	Phony Stocks	*SM*	*10*	*J/D*	*XXXX*

We sat there in silence for several years.

"So what are we looking for?" Catsby said slowly.

"Gee, if I knew, I'd've solved it by now. What's the first thing you notice?"

"It comes out even." Catsby was counting the lines on the screen. "There are six on the one side and six on the other."

"A good observation," I said, "which allows me to hope they're related."

"Related how?"

"That remains the question," I said. "And aside from the two rows of sixes, I haven't a clue."

I squinted in silence.

"You're looking for what?"

"For something in common. I thought for a while it would be the initials that started the code, but there's no HR for a Harold Rigby and no TT for a Tippi Tapp. Keep watching the screen," I said. "Look for connections."

"Among the initials?"

"Wherever," I said.

"I'll take the initials but nothing connects. I see an SH and I see a BB and I see—"

"You're a genius!" I said. "That's it!"

Catsby looked startled.

"Look at the poem."

"For a genuine genius, I seem to be dumb."

"Look at it closely and what do you see? Shot Husband. SH. Burned Building. BB. It seems to be working."

"Except for the X."

"The X," I decided, "is Zelda Stardust."

"His ex-girlfriend?"

"Or ex-hope."

"And the TP?"

"Is for Total Phony."

"Or Ted Parker?"

"You're right again. If Rex knew the secret, he knew the name. Now look at it *this* way." I copied the verse and then jiggered the order:

Harold Rigby	Burned Building	*BB*	*15*	*M/S*	*XXXXX*
Tippi Tapp	Stole Mings	*SM*	*10*	*J/D*	*XXXX*
Mona Fragg	Shot Husband	*SH*	*10*	*J/J*	*XXXXX*
Zelda Stardust	Did Things	*X*	*2*	*F/A*	*XXXXX*
Catsby's roommate	Total Phony	*TP*	*5*	*A/O*	*XXXXX*
Marlon Maykout	Phony Stocks	*PS*	*20*	*M/N*	*XXXX*

Catsby applauded. Catsby said, "Hah!" Catsby was sitting on Hunnicker's hairbrush, jiggling gently and having some fun, getting auto tummy rubs all by himself. "So we've solved the mystery. Brilliant," he said.

"Easy, Sherlock. We've far from done it."

"We haven't done it?"

I said, "Not yet. We've only confirmed who he put in the book. Or *maybe* confirmed who he put in the book. But what are the x's, the ones at the end? Sometimes it's five of them, sometimes it's four. And what are the numbers? And what are the letters with slashes between them?"

"I see what you mean." Catsby dismounted from Hunnicker's brush. "So we haven't entirely broken the code."

"And we're not any closer to clearing Ted."

"Are you saying it's over?"

"It isn't over until it's over. You better go home. Pansy'll need you. You'll need some dinner." I closed the computer. "And so will I."

116

22

"So *there's* our kitten," the Sister cooed. (Do I look like a kitten? I'm seven years old. And the sound of her cooing was sand in my ears.) But I wanted dinner. I rubbed her leg. She thought it was personal. What a fool. Hunnicker rose from his chair like a gallant. "He wants his supper," he said with a grunt and left for the kitchen. I sat on his chair. It gave me an eye-level look at the screen where the 6 o'clock newsman was doing his thing. Trouble in Asia. Trouble in Greece. A storm in Chicago. Hunnicker laughed as he entered the room again, holding a plate. "He always does that," he said to his sister. "He likes to sit in a warmed-over chair."

"And you always let him."

"I guess I do." He put the plate on the seat of the chair. It was chicken and carrots in some kind of sauce. He sat on the sofa. I ate my meal. The 6 o'clock newsman was babbling on and then suddenly: *"Murder in East Ham. A famous author is part of the plot. But first, the weather."* I held my breath (but I kept on eating; a meal is a meal) and then after a while a woman came on.

"This is Sadie Sanders on Long Island where local police have been dragging the bay

(shot of police who were dragging the bay)

"in search of the body of Rex Trout, the notorious gossip and noted author. His house had been ransacked and shots had been fired, and it wasn't surprising to Mrs. Krapotkin who cleans his cottage and shared her fears."

(Shot of an nice-looking middle-aged woman who seemed to be weeping.)

"I knew it," she said. *"I knew it the second I looked at the flounder. I knew he'd be murdered. The same as the duck."*

The reporter explained about flounders and ducks and how Mrs. Krapotkin had happened to find them on serial Saturdays, days that she cleaned.

The scene was then changed to the front of the courthouse, where "J.J. Smythington" covered his face as a squadron of cameras flashed in his eyes. The reporter reported that *"J.J. Smythington, simply described as a person of interest, was questioned at lunchtime but left to go home. And we'll bring you the rest as the story unfolds."*

Cut to commercial. Hunnicker's sister said, "Isn't that awful," and Hunnicker shrugged and said, "What's for dinner?" The sister said, "Steak, if you'll put on the charcoal."

The two of them left.

The commercial in progress had scenes of an island, with plenty of palm trees and frolicking surf. Someone was singing a tropical tune:

Fly to Tahiti.
It's where you belong.
Lovely Tahiti.
Yours for a song.

The song started fading. A shot of the sun was replaced by a stylized globe of the world that was greenish and blueish and sprouted some wings and the gold-speckled letters of GLOBAL AIRLINES and, right underneath it, THE WINGS OF THE WORLD.

I sat for a second and stared at the screen—at the fine-feathered image of globe-sprouting-wings. And I suddenly got it. It came in a flash. The thousands of pieces came crashing together. I knew who had done it. I also knew how. But I still had to prove it.

I leapt from my chair.

"Hey! Whoa! Stop! Halt! HOLD it!" Tom snapped. "Unless you're running from a dog." He looked around nervously as Flo hid behind him. We'd practically collided in the middle of Hunnicker's yard as I'd been rocketing towards the road and now I barked at him rather impatiently that No, there was no dog, "except I'm really quite in a hurry now to-"

"Cancel it," Tom said. " We came all the way over here to tell you something important so the least you can do is listen." He glanced back at Flo and said, "Honeybun, tell it."

Flo said, "You're *certain* there aren't any dogs?"

I said I was certain.

"Absolutely?"

"If you haven't seen a dog then he isn't there. So go on," I said assuringly, "What's it all about?"

"Oh," she said, "Well...it's about Mrs. Rolf. The

doctor's receptionist? Also his nurse? The one he said was planning to be away for the whole weekend? Well, she wasn't. She cut it short. She had this screamy-fight with her sister. So this morning she sees the doctor and she tells him about the fight and then he asks her about the blood."

"Rex's blood," Tom clarified. "The blood that was in the office and supposedly went to the lab?"

"So she says to him, '*What* blood?' She says, 'There *wasn't* any blood.' And then the doctor says, 'I took about an armful from Mr. Trout.' And then she tells him it wasn't there, and then he snaps at her, 'Did you *look*?' and then she tells him Of *course* she looked, and then he says to her, 'Think again. You didn't take the blood to the lab?' And then she looks at him. 'Oh my goodness, you're like my sister,' she says, and leaves."

I thought it over. "And you believe her?"

"Absolutely." She nodded twice.

I started grinning. The crazy puzzle was making sense to me. Wonderful sense. "I hate to leave you," I said, "but now I really —"

Voices shattered the air. Dozens of voices, yowling at once and they seemed to be coming from Catsby's hedges.

"*We want justice!*" the voices yowled, as Catsby and Pansy burst through the hedge.

"What's going on?" I said over the uproar.

"Come and look at it," Catsby said.

23

Adozen people with four-foot sticks that had cardboard signs on them circled the pool. They were marching around it while other people were under the windows and howling in.

"Hey-Hey-Hey!" they were chanting together. I looked at the posters that sat on the sticks.

One said: **DOWN WITH THE UPPER CLASS.**

One said: **UP WITH THE DOWNER CLASS.**

A pizza delivery man held a sign that said **NO JUSTICE, NO PIZZA!** while somebody else's said **JUSTICE FOR ALL!** and a trio of posters said **PIZZA FOR ALL!** and another one added, **NO GARLIC ON MINE!**

A pretty lady with auburn hair and a scribbled sign that said **SOAK THE RICH!** was delightedly tossing a chair in the pool. And, after the chair, came a potted petunia, and after the plant came a marble frog. *Splash!Splash!* The water went everywhere.

Pansy was frightened. Catsby was grim. We hid in the hedges, protected by leaves, as the chanting grew louder and notably meaner and two more petunias ker-plunked in the pool.

"Hey! Hey! Jay! Jay!
Who did you toss in the bay today?"

"Hey! Hey! Jay! Jay!
We're gonna get you and make you pay!"

"This is horribly dangerous," Flo said tightly.

"They're out of control now," I said. "They're a mob."

"But what are they after?"

"Attention," I said, as a couple of vans that were marked with the letters of popular networks had screeched to a halt and reporters came out of them, cameras in hand. They rushed to the poolside and started to shoot.

The gang at the pool had grown louder and louder. The pointless destruction was painful to see. Catsby's playroom, uprooted and trashed. A magnificent rose bush, uprooted and splashed. And the shouting continued:

Jay! Jay!
We're gonna get you and make you pay!

"But what are they angry at?" Pansy whispered. "He didn't do it. So why should he pay? And none of these idiots knew Mr. Trout. I don't understand it."

"It's not about Trout." I looked at the looters.

"Then what's it about?"

"It's more about pizza," I said.

"You're joking."

"I'm partly joking. It's all about stuff. It's what J.J. has and the rest of them don't. And they want to

122

have it."

"Then why do they trash it?"

"Because they don't have it."

Tom shook his head. "They're like dogs in the manger."

"They're haters," I said. "And it seems at the moment, they're hating the rich. And it's just as disgusting as hating the poor. Or the old, or the young, or the black or the white. It's a rotten routine and it's always the same. They put people in groups and then hate them in groups and forget that they're people."

Catsby looked sad. "You mean it's like people who say they hate cats. They just hate us in general. Hate us on sight. And like nobody cares that we're all very different and most of us friendly."

"Exactly," I said.

"But you're missing the obvious," Tom butted in, "because some of these rich folks are totally scum."

I looked at him thoughtfully. "So are some cats. And so's some of everyone. Wealthy or poor. And most of the crooks that I've known weren't rich. And most of the rich folks I've known weren't crooks. But just look at these violent idiot jerks. They clamor for justice while being unjust. They holler for fairness while being unfair. And look at these guys from the networks enjoy them. They ought to get angry and call the police."

Instead, they were setting up chats with the looters who'd taken to stealing the tables and chairs and were prying the tiles from the edge of the pool. I'd suddenly had it. I got an idea.

"All right," I said softly. "I'm counting to three and we go into action. Is everyone cool?"

Catsby was nodding. Pansy was cleverly honing her claws on the edge of a stone. Flo said, "I'm ready," and Tom said, "*Three!*"

We raced from the hedges and out to the pool where the tiles that were left had turned sloshingly wet and as slick as an ice rink. I'd counted on that.

We leapt at the looters and tugged at their cuffs till they slipped in their sandals and splashed to the pool. The guy who'd demanded **NO GARLIC ON MINE!** tumbled into a camera that tilted and slid as the cameraman dove for it, missing the tiles and went into the swimming pool, landing, ker-splash on the thorns of the rose bush as **PIZZA FOR ALL!** did a beautiful bellyflop onto his head and the two of them sunk and then bobbed to the surface with bits of petunia entwined in their hair, as the redheaded lady who'd thrown the first chair tumbled into the newsguy from CNN as the newsgirl from Fox stumbled into a table that hadn't been stolen and tripped on the tile that supported the redhead who grabbed for the newsguy who totally lost it and fell to the pool with the redhead beside him, along with her sign that proclaimed, rather comically, **SOAK THE RICH!**

By then, it was over. The pool was an ocean of splashing bodies and soggy signs and whoever was left in the garden had fled.

"I think," Catsby said, as we watched from the hedges, "I think we did justice."

"I think," Tom decided, "I think we had fun." He looked at me grinning. "And how about you?"

"I think it went swimmingly."

Everyone laughed.

124

24

I wandered away in pursuit of my errand while everyone else stayed to clean up the mess, retrieving the
treasures from Catsby's toy chest and putting them
tenderly back in their place as Ted and Zelda came out
of the house.

I ran through the woods in the gathering twilight
and made it to Rex's in pretty good time. The air in
the cottage was stale and musty— the odor of silence
and weeksful of dust. I went to the den again, finding
the page that we'd torn from the notebook, the page
with the code. I looked at the lines that had always
perplexed me:

10	*J/J*	*X X X X X*
2	*F/A*	*X X X X X*
15	*M/S*	*X X X X X*
5	*A/O*	*X X X X X*
20	*M/N*	*X X X X*
10	*J/D*	*X X X X*

I looked at what Rex had once penciled above them: his *Desperation!* his *Utter despair!* Words that he'd written when words had failed him. When writing a sentence exceeded his skill. When talent had fled and his wit couldn't catch it. And where did that leave him? It left him in debt. What he owed was a manuscript— thousands of words— or the half-million dollars he'd taken to write it, which, failing to write it, he'd have to return.

Did he even have it? I thought he didn't. I figured he'd blown it on buying the house not to mention the Lexus and everything else. And I also remembered what Pansy'd told me—that Rex had been swindled by Phony Stocks (or as Pansy had put it, that Marlon Maykout had left him a drawerful of "broken socks.") And that, plus the meaning of the globe-sprouting-wings, added up to the answer.

I raced to the desk. I opened the drawer with the plastic checkbook and pawed once again through the ink-scribbled stubs.

+ $10,000 in January;
+ $2,000 in February;
+ $15,000 in March;
+ $5,000 in April.

I held my excitment and looked at the code.

+ $10,000 in January	10	J/J
+ $2,000 in February	2	F/A
+ $15,000 in March	15	M/S
+ $5,000 in April	5	A/O

I looked at the numbers again and the letters—the ones before and after the slash. The "10" in the code stood for $10,000 and the "J" before the slash stood for

January (J). And it followed down the list. February (F), March (M), April (A) and the rest of the letters—

$$20 \quad M/N$$
$$10 \quad J/D$$

—took us neatly into June. And if logic were a part of it, the second set of letters, the letters behind the slash, would be the opening letters of the final months of the year. I checked them out carefully. Yup. That was it.

The people who Rex had been outing in his book had been paying him blackmail to *not* write his book. Or to not include *them*. But the joke, in its awfulness, was also on them. Because the truth was, he couldn't write the book if he tried. And he'd certainly tried. Those notebooks and notebooks full of dumb, pointless words. And his failure to write it led to *Utter Despair.* And to plotting the blackmail.

I stared at the code. And this time I focused on the column at the left and put the whole thing together:

SH	10	J/J	XXXXX
X	2	F/A	XXXXX
BB	15	M/S	XXXXX
TP	5	A/O	XXXXX
PS	20	M/N	XXXX
SM	10	J/D	XXXX

SH— Shot Husband— paid $10,000 in Jan and July.

X—Zelda, who didn't want her high school picture in the news: $2,000 two times a year.

BB— Harold Rigby— $15,000 in March and September.

TP—Ted Parker— $5000 in April/October.

After that, there was May. PS (Marlon Maykout)

owed a bundle to Rex in May but he apparently hadn't paid it. Or he hadn't paid it yet. But then late on the Saturday of May 29th, Mr. Maykout, in hot panic, came a-knocking at Rex's door, going "Rex, I haven't forgotten!"

Forgotten what?

To pay the tab.

And now even the x's here were suddenly making sense. The x's stood for times. Meaning how many times they'd paid. Four x's, four times. Which would mean that the little blackmail scheme had lasted for two years. And, for some of them, two-and-a-half.

I applauded my own brain. It was, after all, for a thing the size of an Easter egg, a pretty remarkable toy. But it knew, in its wisdom, that it still had to gather proof. Without the proof, what it knew was useless.

I began to search for the proof. I started finding it, poring slowly through the papers from Rex's bank. I was getting groggy.

The telephone rang.

Rex's message haunted the air—a ghostly version of "Do your thing."

A voice in the distance said, "Wrong number."

The wakened machine then proceded to blink—an amber light going on and off and reporting the number of calls was 4, including the last one. I hated the blink. I pressed on a button to make it stop, but I'd pressed on the wrong one. I'd pressed on the button that replayed the messages starting with 1. And there was the answer—the beautiful message confirming my instinct and wrapping the case.

"Um...Mr. *Fish?*" said a cheerful woman who sported a vaguely exotic accent. "I'm calling from the

Tiki Hotel in Tahiti. I'm confirming that our car picks you up at the airport meeting Flight 27 from Global Airlines, arriving Tahiti on Sunday afternoon. Have a very nice trip, sir. We see you then soon."

The machine then obligingly time-stamped the message. "Saturday," it said in its mechanical mumble, and added, "At 11:57 AM."

While Rex was at the doctor's. While I was in the woods. While Georgia was languidly listening to Pansy as the two of them nestled on the cushions of the couch.

I raced back to Hunnicker's, charging through the woods.

25

"Some buddy," Catsby said as I pounded past his hedge. "When it comes to the clean-up time, you're nowhere to be found."

I grinned at him. "Catsby, I was cleaning up the case."

"You were?" he said. "Really?"

"I'll explain it all later. Give me time to write it down." I glanced rather anxiously at Hunnicker's driveway. It was empty. Meaning Hunnicker and Company were gone. "Come around in twenty minutes. Bring everyone," I said.

It was quiet in the house. Hunnicker's laptop was sleeping on the bed, meaning all I had to do was raise the lid and it awoke. I typed in my password and again found the e-mail I'd sent myself from Nosey's. I owed him the story. I'd promised him a total exclusive on the case and I knew he'd pass it on. The reporters would get it and so would the police. I hit the Reply tab and flew across the keys.

Catsby arrived first, Pansy second, Tom, third. "Wait for Flo," he said. "She wanted to freshen up, if you know what I mean."

"I hope she buries it," Pansy said.

"Of *course* she buries it." Tom replied. He looked offended. He also noted that Catsby's paw was on Pansy's back as they lay together atop the bedspread. Tom leapt up on the other side.

There was awkward silence. I cleared my throat.

"Do you want to tell him?" I said to Pansy. I glanced from Pansy to Catsby to Tom. "I mean...if you'd like, I can leave the room."

"Tell him *what*?" she said. "Oh my goodness!" It suddenly dawned and she added, "That. Um...Tom?" She looked at him meltingly. "Tom— this is terribly hard and I wouldn't hurt you for all the world, but the total fact of it is that Catsby and I— forgive me, Tom— we're in love and I've promised to—"

"Marry him?" Tom was grinning. "But that's sensational, Pansy. Gee. I mean it's wonderful. Isn't it, Sam?"

I cocked my head at him.

Pansy frowned. "I thought at least you'd be decently hurt."

Tom grew sober. He said, "I am. I'm horribly wounded. Honest," he said. "You're the prettiest lady I ever dated. You're also the sweetest," he said, "by far. But, face it, Pansy, we've nothing in common. You always knew it. And so did I."

She nodded thoughtfully. "Yes, I did. You were very kind to me, Tom. You were. I was totally lost when

131

we moved to the country. You gave me friendship. You gave me comfort. You're like ... a brother."

He nodded. "Right. And you're like a sister." He grinned at Flo who had suddenly burst through the bedroom door. "Come up here and sit with me, Flo," he said. She leapt to the pillow and settled beside him. Tom put his paw on the back of her hip.

It was all so cozy I started to wonder if this was a love story, after all, and not just a mystery.

"Ready?" I said. I swiveled the laptop and tapped at the screen, "Why don't you read it. I'll answer questions when everyone's finished."

They started to read:

Exclusive to Ham Herald (Please forward to Police.)
FISH STORY
FAILED AUTHOR FAKES HIS OWN DEATH

"*What!?*" Pansy argued.
"Just read it," I said.
They read:

Rex Trout wasn't murdered. Rex Trout isn't dead. He left for Tahiti on Global Airlines, on Flight 27 on Saturday night. You'll find him right now at the Tiki Hotel as the message on his answering machine will confirm. He seems to be going by the name Mr. Fish.

Don't be fooled by the "crime scene." Rex wasn't shot. In fact, Rex was the shooter. Or, to put that another way, he shot his own clock He seems to have done it at about 2 PM after jiggering the hands to read 5:41. After that, for the fun of it, he shot his own wall. The gun he was shooting with was J.J. Smythington's— a gun that he'd stolen at a party April 1st. where he'd also...

Catsby suddenly read aloud to me, " '...*stole the shoes!*'—But what a genius you are," he said. "But how did you know he was at the party?"

"Well he was," I said, "wasn't he?"

"Yes. But how did you know?"

"Because you told me," I said flatly. "You told Pansy but I was there. You said Rex had come over to a party on April Fool's and you'd been hoping he'd bring Pansy."

"What a memory!" Pansy said.

"I'm part elephant."

"No you're not."

"Then how do you think I got to be gray? But keep reading," I said. "Please."

They turned their attentions back to the screen:

The blood at the crime scene was definitely Rex's (as I'm sure you're about to learn) except it wasn't shed at the scene. It's the blood from the doctor's office. He'd faked an illness to see the doctor to get the doctor to take his blood which he'd fully intended on taking back. It was actually pretty easy.

Once the doctor had left his office, Rex returned with the lame excuse that he'd left his glasses, and grabbed the blood.

"Oh my goodness!" Flo was astounded now. "So *that's* how it disappeared. Well, goodness gracious!" she babbled again. "Who'd ever have guessed it?"

"My cousin Sam, that's who'd've guessed it. In fact, he did. He's extremely brilliant," Pansy informed her. "It runs in the family."

Catsby laughed.

"Would you keep on reading?" I said.

They read:

So back at the cottage, he trashed his office

"But why would he do that?" Tom was perplexed.

"To make it appear that the book had been burgled. I wish you'd read this," I said, "but listen, it's pretty simple. He dribbled his blood from the clock to the hallway and onto the rug. The rug by the cat-door? The one in the back?"

"It's the little oval one," Pansy added. "I always liked it. It's totally soft."

"I can tell you the rest of it," Catsby offered. "He dragged the rug to his own little boat—"

"Wearing J.J.'s sneakers," I said. "He had to leave J.J.'s footprints." I tapped the screen at the part where I'd written

in J.J's sneakers

"Oh man, can I finish it?" Catsby complained. "It's the story you told me the night of the crime. That he rowed with the rug in the boat to the bay and he dumped all the evidence."

"Lovely," I said. "But I didn't know all of it. Not at the time. And I sure didn't figure the 'killer' was Rex."

"Well, you *practically* knew it."

I didn't fight. If you want to believe I'm an absolute genius, I'll let you believe it.

"So what happened then?" Pansy was puzzled.

"He scuttled the rowboat and swam to the shore."
"But what happened *then*?" she insisted sharply.
"Read," I commanded
She sighed and read:

> After that, it's a little hazy. He might have
> had a waterproof backpack that held his stuff—
> the stuff he needed to finish the job. The stuff in
> question being a hoodie, a funky wig, and a pair
> of shoes, and, of course, his ticket for Global
> Airlines. Somewhere or other, perhaps in the
> forest, he must have hidden his rented bike,
> and he got on the bike and he rode into town.
> You'll find the bike—it's a screaming yellow—
> parked at the side of the Ham Hotel, where Rex
> had a room as a Mr. McGee—-"

"The Mysterious Stranger!" Tom clapped his paws.
"The Mysterious Stranger was Rex all along?"
I nodded slowly. "He planned it well. But they'll
still find his fingerprints all through the room and, of
course, on the bicycle."
Catsby frowned. "But why was he faking his
murder at all?"
"Would you keep on reading?" I said.
They read.

> He picked up the bags that he'd left at the
> Ham and then got on the 4 o'clock bus to New
> York and then went to the airport. Along the
> way, he telephoned J.J., promised the gun, and
> then set up a date in the Featherstone Woods.
> Why did he do it? To frame J.J.— the fellow he
> figured had stolen his girl.

135

As for the novel— he never wrote it, The only "book" was an empty box. But he faked it to look like the book had been stolen. Instead of writing, he'd taken to crime. The crime was blackmail. It paid him well. Take a look at the papers you'll find from his bank and they'll show you the trail of suspicious deposits. Look at the page full of code on his desk. Put them together and look what you've got: A trail of blackmailing, twice a year from a half-dozen people. You're wondering who? Look for the people who <u>S</u>hot their <u>H</u>usbands and <u>B</u>urned their <u>B</u>uildings and <u>S</u>tole their <u>M</u>ings, which are otherwise vases. And while you're up, look at Marlon Maykout, whose <u>P</u>hony <u>S</u>tocks have been bleeding millions for several years. Figure they're guilty or why would they pay?

Yours in detection, (and very sincerely),
Sam The Cat, Private Eye

Pansy was a gasping. "Oh my goodness! You actually signed with your actual *name?*"

"What does it matter?" I started laughing. "They'd never believe that it came from a cat."

"They underrate us." Tom shook his head. "They give us kibble but no respect."

"But this is incredible," Catsby said. "And the best part of all is, you're clearing Ted."

Pansy looked up at him. "Who's Ted?"

"Did I say *Ted?* What I meant was…Jed. As in Jedediah," he offered nimbly. "It's one of J.J's incredible J's. I forget the other one."

"Probably John," Flo said reflectively.

Tom tapped the screen. "There's a hole in your story." He tapped it again. "You're saying at first it's a half-dozen people— which adds up to six— but you only name four. Or actually one, but you hint at the others. So who are the rest of them?"

"Gee, I don't know." I looked over at Catsby. "And no one will guess. And Rex, if they catch him, won't spill any beans because four counts of blackmail are surely enough."

Catsby said nothing but sighed his relief.

"I still have a question." Pansy was frowning. "About the flounder, I mean, and the duck.— How did they get there?"

"An excellent question. Of course he planted them there by himself. And he always planted them Saturday mornings so Mrs. Krapotkin would find them and scream. And she'd tell the police and they'd think he was threatened."

"An evil genius." Flo shook her head.

"Not such a genius," I added dryly. "He left all the evidence right in his desk."

Tom looked up at me. "What now?"

"Now we wait," I said, "for the cops. They'll solve it nicely. I'd say tomorrow or maybe Tuesday. We'll watch the news."

"But it's you who solved it!" Pansy was miffed. "And you'll never get credit. It isn't fair!"

"But we'll never change that," Flo said serenely. "We just accept it and know what we know. And the credit aside," she said, smiling sweetly, "there's quite an advantage in playing dumb. It's like when they're telling you, 'Stay off the sofa'? You just go blank like you don't understand. *No comprende. No kapish.*

No speak English. See what I mean?"

"I never thought of that," Pansy said.

"Well, you ought to try it. Works like a charm. I was saying to Tommy—"

The door burst open and Hunnicker's sister was starting to shriek. *"What are you doing? Get off the bedspread! Get off the pillow! GET OFF THE BED!!"*

We looked at her blankly and didn't budge.

26

I spent the night in the woods with Virgil. Catsby had Pansy and Tom had Flo but I had Virgil— a cranky coot who was almost the father I'd never had but had always wanted. I told him the tale about Rex's "murder" and how it was planned and he patted my paw and said, "Nicely, nicely. You done that nicely. I'm proud a ya, Slick."

We climbed to his treetop and hid in its branches and watched all the lights going off in the town and then off in the houses, and looked at the moon as it rose in the heavens. We talked through the night. We talked about everything, not speaking words, but just thinking in silence and passing it on. At one point he grunted and said, "That was funny."

"I'm glad it amused you," I said.

We napped. At one point we woke and I asked him, word-wise, if ever he'd had any human home.

"Got some folks down on Bayside. They live in a cottage. They give me my suppers and leave me alone and if ever it's snowing or raining hardballs, I sleep in their kitchen. I figure they're mine if I wanted to have 'em," he said. "But I don't. But if ever I died at the top of my tree house, I figure they'd find me and dig me a grave."

"Would you not talk of dying?" I said.

"Why not? You know everyone does it. An angel comes down and she whispers 'It's time now,' and everyone goes. Gotta figure it's best if you're not being murdered or hit by a streetcar, or something like that, but I bet they got treetops and maybe a rainbow and plenty of catnip, so what's all the fuss?"

"Would you keep in touch with me?"

"What? From heaven?"

"I'd changed the subject. I meant from Ham. I could e-mail Nosey who'd give you message?"

"I'd like your message. If Nosey'd bring it. I ain't one for travelin much into town."

"I can understand that," I said. "I wish I could e-mail catnip. I'd send you an ounce."

"Only an ounce?" he said. "Man, you slickers is some kind a stingy."

We both had a laugh. And then soon after laughing, we both fell asleep.

I got back to Hunnicker's just before noon. He looked at me crossly and said, "Where were *you*?"

I wasn't in love with his tone or his manner. His arms were folded and covered his chest and I noticed his luggage was packed and zippered and standing erect on the kitchen floor.

"Come on. We're leaving," he said. "I've had it. She threw a fit about cats on the bed and your bringing your pals to her clean little house and she smelled cigarette smoke on one of the curtains. On one of the *curtains.* Imagine *that*! So I said to her, 'Tillie— if curtains and bedspreads are much more important than brothers and cats, then I'll just have to pity you. Never again! Never again will I visit your house!'" He glanced at the hallway. "She's up in her bedroom and cleaning like crazy, so let's get it on." He picked up his luggage and lifted me up like a sack of potatoes and stalked to the car.

Catsby was watching. "You're being *carried*?" he said in amazement. I jumped to the ground. Hunnicker yelled at me. Catsby said, "Better. What's with your human?" I told him "They fought. It's what families do on a holiday weekend. They fight with their sisters and leave in a huff."

Hunnicker hollered, "I'm counting to twelve!"

"I gather you're leaving."

I nodded. "Yeah. Give my love to Pansy," I said. "I'm sure you'll take wonderful care of her."

"Yes, I will."

"Have you got my e-mail?" He said he didn't. I spelled it out for him. "Stay in touch."

Hunicker hollered, "I'm counting to twenty!"

I trotted with dignity into the car.

And that's how it happened that, four hours later, I sat in the office of Hunnicker's bookstore with Sue on the blotter and me on the chair, while I told her the story.

She looked in my eyes. "That was some vacation," she said. "You worked like an absolute dog and you didn't get paid."

"But I got satisfaction," I said.

"Can you eat it?"

"What?"

"Satisfaction."

I said, "You've a point. But I can't say I've solved it till Trout has been caught, and confessed that he did it, and Ted has been cleared." I looked at the clock on the wall of the office. I looked at the Sony across from the desk. It was practically time for the six o'clock news. I pawed the remote on, and settled with Sue on the edge of the blotter.

We watched a parade. It was, I remembered, a special weekend. A weekend to celebrate wonderful people who'd fought for the country, and fought for our rights. We looked at the flags and the hundreds of marchers. We looked at the soldiers. We looked at the crowds and we listened to speeches, or parts of speeches, from several mayors from several towns, who were so full of blather, we practically screamed.

And then came the teaser that grabbed our attention. "Author captured on tropical isle." We held our breaths now and stared at the screen as the footage unfolded. Trout on the hook—handcuffed and marched from the Tiki Hotel to a waiting police car. "Wanted on several charges of blackmail," the newsman intoned, "and for framing his neighbor, and stealing his pistol, and also for plotting to fake his own death. An anonymous tipster alerted police but he signed his message—" the newsman tittered— "he signed his message as Sam The Cat."

"An incredible kitty," the newsgirl giggled.

"Here, kitty-kitty," the newsguy purred.

"Would you just turn it off now?" Sue'd gotten

angry. "I hate their laughing. Why do they laugh?"

"But the laugh's on *them*," I said, snuggling closer. "Besides, every cat in the city will know, and they'll give me their business."

The telephone rang.

"Is this Sam, the detective?" a kitten cooed. "I lost my collar. It's made of rubies and several diamonds and several pearls, and I saw on the news you're a brilliant detective so—"

"Call me tomorrow," I said. "After six. At the moment I'm busy."

I hung up the phone.

I looked up at Sue who said, "What are you thinking?"

"I'm thinking I missed you," I said. "Shall we dance?"

About the Author

LINDA STEWART HAS WRITTEN 17 ADULT CRIME NOVELS AND FILM NOVELIZATIONS PLUS TELEVISION DRAMAS AND DOCUMENTARIES. *SAM THE CAT: DETECTIVE*, HER FIRST BOOK FOR CHILDREN, WAS INSPIRED BY HER LIVE-IN CAT, NAMED SAM, WHO GENEROUSLY LETS HER SHARE HIS MANHATTAN APARTMENT. THE FIRST BOOK IN THE SERIES (THAT NOW NUMBERS FOUR) WAS NOMINATED FOR THE MYSTERY WRITERS OF AMERICA'S EDGAR AWARD; THE THIRD WAS NOMINATED FOR THE AGATHA AWARD AND WON THE MUSE AWARD (BEST JUVENILE FICTION)..

About Sam

YOU CAN READ AN INTERVIEW WITH SAM HIMSELF (CONDUCTED BY GINGER PEACH, THE FELINE ASSOCIATE EDITOR OF *CATALOG* MAGAZINE) IF YOU GO TO SAM'S WEBSITE, WWW.SAMTHECAT.COM. HE WELCOMES QUESTIONS FROM READERS AND YOU CAN E-MAIL HIM THROUGH HIS SITE, OR WRITE TO HIM CARE OF THE PUBLISHER.

TO GET PERSONALLY AUTOGRAPHED COPIES
OR TO LEARN WHEN SAM'S NEXT BOOK WILL BE AVAILABLE
send a letter or postcard to
Cheshire House Books
P.O. Box 2484, New York City, NY 10021
or look for Sam's website:
HTTP://WWW.SAMTHECAT.COM

CPSIA information can be obtained at www.ICGtesting.com
Printed in the USA
BVOW03s1953170614

356598BV00001B/5/P